Ladies Must Live

Ladies Must Live

Alice Duer Miller

MINT EDITIONS

Ladies Must Live was first published in 1917.

This edition published by Mint Editions 2021.

ISBN 9781513283609 | E-ISBN 9781513288628

Published by Mint Editions®

 MINT
EDITIONS

minteditionbooks.com

Publishing Director: Jennifer Newens
Design & Production: Rachel Lopez Metzger
Project Manager: Micaela Clark
Typesetting: Westchester Publishing Services

Contents

I   7

II   24

III   41

IV   60

V   80

VI   98

I

Mrs. Ussher was having a small house party in the country over New Year's Day. This is equivalent to saying that the half dozen most fashionable people in New York were out of town.

Certain human beings are admitted to have a genius for discrimination in such matters as objects of art, pigs or stocks. Mrs. Ussher had this same instinct in regard to fashion, especially where fashions in people were concerned. She turned toward hidden social availability very much as the douser's hazel wand turns toward the hidden spring. When she crossed the room to speak to some woman after dinner, whatever that woman's social position might formerly have been, you could be sure that at present she was on the upward wing. When Mrs. Ussher discovered extraordinary qualities of mind and sympathy in some hitherto impossible man, you might be certain it was time to begin to book him in advance.

Not that Mrs. Ussher was a kingmaker; she herself had no more power over the situation than the barometer has over the weather. She merely was able to foretell; she had the sense of approaching social success.

She was unaware of her own powers, and really supposed that her sudden and usually ephemeral friendships were based on mutual attraction. The fact that for years her friends had been the small group of the momentarily fashionable required, in her eyes, no explanation. So simple was her creed that she believed people were fashionable for the same reason that they were her friends, because "they were so nice."

During the short period of their existence, Mrs. Ussher gave to these friendships the utmost loyalty and devotion. She agonized over the financial, domestic and romantic troubles of her friends; she sat up till the small hours, talking to them like a schoolgirl; during the height of their careers she organized plots for their assistance; and even when their stars were plainly on the decline, she would often ask them to lunch, if she happened to be alone.

Many people, we know, are prone to make friends with the rich and great. Mrs. Ussher's genius consisted in having made friends with them before they were either. When you hurried to her with some account of a newly discovered treasure—a beauty or a conversable young man—she would always say: "Oh, yes, I crossed with her two years ago," or "Isn't he a dear?—he was once in Jack's office." The strange thing was these statements were always true; the subjects of them confessed with tears that "dear Mrs. Ussher" or "darling Laura" was the kindest friend they had ever had.

Her house party was therefore likely to be notable.

First, there was of course Mrs. Almar—of course without her husband. There is only one thing, or perhaps two, to be said for Nancy Almar—that she was very handsome and that she was not a hypocrite, no more than a pirate is a hypocrite who comes aboard with his cutlass in his teeth. Mrs. Almar's cutlass was always in her teeth, when it was not in somebody's vitals.

She had smooth, jet-black hair, done close to her pretty head, a clear white-and-vermilion complexion, and a good figure, not too tall. She said little, but everything she did say, she most poignantly meant. If, while you were talking to her, she suddenly cried out: "Ah, that's really good!" there was no doubt you had had the good fortune to amuse her; while if she yawned and left you in the midst of a sentence there was no question that she was bored.

She hated her husband—not for the conventional reason that she had married him. She hated him because he was a hypocrite, because he was always placating and temporizing.

For instance, he had said to her as she was about to start for the Usshers':

"I hope you'll explain to them why I could not come."

There had never been the least question of Mr. Almar's coming, and she turned slowly and looked at him as she asked:

"You mean that I would not have gone if you had?"

He did not seem annoyed.

"No," he said, "that I'm called South on business."

"I shan't tell them that," she said, slowly wrapping her furs about her throat; and then foreseeing a comic moment, she added, "but I'll tell them you say so, if you like."

She was as good as her word—she usually was.

When the party was at tea about the drawing-room fire, she asked without the slightest change of expression:

"Would any one like to hear Roland's explanation of why he is not with us?"

"Had it anything to do with his not being asked?" said a pale young man; and as soon as he had spoken, he glanced hastily round the circle to ascertain how his remark had succeeded.

ALICE DUER MILLER

So far as Mrs. Almar was concerned it had not succeeded at all, in fact, though he did not know it, nothing he said would ever succeed with her again, although a week before she had hung upon his every word. He had been a new discovery, something unknown and Bohemian, but alas, a day or two before, she had observed that underlying his socialistic theories was an aching desire for social recognition. He liked to tell his bejeweled hostesses about his friends the car-drivers; but, oh, twenty times more, he would have liked to tell the car-drivers about his friends the bejeweled hostesses. For this reason Mrs. Almar despised him, and where she despised she made no secret of the fact.

"Not asked, Mr. Wickham!" she said. "I assume my husband is asked wherever I am," and then turning to Laura Ussher she added with a faint smile: "One's husband is always asked, isn't he?"

"Certainly, as long as you never allow him to come," said another speaker.

This was the other great beauty of the hour—or, since she was blond and some years younger than Mrs. Almar, perhaps it would be right to say that she was the beauty of the hour.

She was very tall, golden, fresh, smooth, yet with faint hollows in her cheeks that kept her freshness from being insipid. Christine Fenimer had another advantage—she was unmarried. In spite of the truth of the observation that a married woman's greatest charm is her husband, he is also in the most practical sense a disadvantage; he does sometimes stand across the road of advancement, even in a land of easy divorce. Mrs. Almar, for instance, was regretfully aware that she might have done much better than Roland Almar. The great stakes were really open to the unmarried.

She was particularly aware of this fact at the moment, for the party was understood to be awaiting a great stake. Mrs. Ussher had discovered a cousin, a young man who, soon after graduating from a technical college, had invented a process in the manufacture of rubber that had brought him a fortune before he was thirty. He was now engaged in spending it on aviation experiments. He was reckless and successful. Besides which he was understood to be personally attractive—his picture in a silver frame stood on a neighboring table. He was of the lean type that Mrs. Almar admired.

Now it was perfectly clear to her why he was asked. Mrs. Ussher adored Christine Fenimer. Of all girls in the world it was essential that Christine should marry money. This man, Max Riatt, new to the fashionable world, ought to be comparatively easy game. The thing ought to go on wheels. But Mrs. Almar herself was not indifferent to six feet of splendid masculinity; nor without her own uses at the moment for a good-looking young man.

In other words, there was going to be a contest; in the full sight of the little public that really mattered, the lists were set. Nobody present, except perhaps Wickham, who was dangerously ignorant of the world in which he was moving, doubted for one moment that Miss Fenimer had resolved to marry Max Riatt, if, that is, he turned out to be actually as per the recommendations of Mrs. Ussher; nor was it less certain that Mrs. Almar intended that he should be hers.

Of course if Mrs. Ussher had been absolutely single-minded, she would not have invited Mrs. Almar to this party; but though a warm friend to Christine Fenimer, Laura was not a fanatic, and the piratical Nancy was her friend, too.

Mrs. Almar could have pleaded an additional reason for her wish to interfere with this match, besides the natural one of not wishing Miss Fenimer to attain any success; and that was the fact that Edward Hickson, her brother, had wanted for several years to marry Christine. Hickson was a dull, kindly, fairly well-to-do young man—exactly the type you would like to see your rival marry. Hickson had motored out with his sister, and had received some excellent counsel on the way.

"Now, Ned," she had said, "don't cut your own throat by being an adoring foil. Don't let Christine grind your face in the dust, just to show this new man that she can do it."

"You don't do Christine justice," he had answered, "if you think she would do that."

His sister did not reply. She thought it would have been doing the girl injustice to suppose that she would do anything else.

They were still sitting about the tea-table at a quarter to seven, when Christine and Mrs. Almar rose simultaneously. It was almost time for the arrival of Riatt, and neither had any fancy for meeting him save at her best—in all the panoply of evening dress.

"We're not dining till a quarter past eight, my dears," said Mrs. Ussher.

Both ladies thought they would lie down before dinner. And here chance took a hand. Riatt's train was late, whereas Christine's clock was fast. And so it happened that she came downstairs just as he was coming up.

ALICE DUER MILLER

There had been no one to greet him. He was told by the butler that Mrs. Ussher was dressing, that dinner would be in fifteen minutes; he started to bound up the stairs, following the footman with his bags, when suddenly looking up the broad flight he saw a blond vision in white and pearls coming slowly down. He hoped that his lower jaw hadn't fallen, but she really was extraordinarily beautiful; and he could not help slowing down a little. She stopped, with her hand on the banisters, like Louise of Prussia.

"Oh, you're Mr. Riatt," she said, very gently. "You know you're most awfully late."

"I wish," he said, "that I were wise enough to be able to say: 'Oh, you're Miss—'"

"I might be a Mrs."

"Oh, I hope not," he answered. "Are you?"

She smiled.

"You'll know as soon as you come down to dinner."

"I shall be quick about dressing."

He went on up, and she pursued her slow progress down. She felt that her future had been settled by those few seconds on the stairs.

"He will do admirably," she said to herself, and a smile like that of a sleeping infant curved her lips. She felt calmly triumphant. She had always said there was no reason why even a rich man should be absolutely impossible. She recalled certain great fortunes with repulsive owners, which some of her friends had accepted. For herself she had always intended to have everything—love and money, too. And here it was, almost in her hands. There had been moments when she had been so discouraged that she had actually made up her mind to marry Ned Hickson. How wise she had been to hold off!

She leant her arm on the mantel-piece and studied herself in the mirror. It was a Chinese painted mirror, and the tint of the glass was green and unbecoming, yet even this could not mar the dazzling reflection. The only object on which she looked with dissatisfaction was her string of pearls; they were imitation. She thought she would have emeralds; and she heard clearly in her own inner ear this sentence: "Yes, that is young Mrs. Max Riatt; is she not very beautiful in her emeralds!"

Fortunately she did not say it aloud, for Mrs. Ussher came down at this moment, and soon Hickson, and then in an incredibly short space of time Riatt himself.

Undoubtedly he would do magnificently. He stood the test even of evening clothes, though Christine fancied as she studied him that she would alter his style of collars. They would be better higher. Mrs. Ussher brought him over at once and introduced him.

"This is my cousin Max, Christine, about whom I've talked so much. Max, this is Miss Fenimer."

They smiled at each other with a common impulse not to confess that earlier meeting on the stairs; and he was just about to settle down beside her, when the door opened and, last of all, Mrs. Almar came in. She was wearing her flame-color and lilac dress. Christine knew she would have it on; knew that she saved it for the greatest moments. She did not advance very far into the room, but stood looking around her.

"Well," she said, "where is Cousin Max?"

It must not be supposed from this question that she had not seen him almost through the crack of the door as the butler opened it for her; but by speaking just when and where she did, she forced him to get up from Christine's side, and come to where she was to be introduced to her. Then as dinner was at the same instant announced, she put her hand on his arm.

"Take me in to dinner, Cousin Max," she said.

"I did not know he was *your* cousin," said Wickham, who suffered from the fatal tendency in moments of doubt to say something.

Mrs. Almar looked at Riatt.

"Will you be a cousin to me?" she asked. "It commits you to nothing."

"I don't consider that an advantage," he returned, drawing his elbow slightly inward, so that her hand, if not actually pressed, was made to feel secure upon his arm. "There are some things I wouldn't a bit mind being committed to."

Mrs. Almar moved her black head from side to side.

"You must be more specific," she said, "or I shan't understand you."

"More specific in words?" he inquired gently. They were crossing the hall, and had a sort of privacy for an instant.

"Dear me," she returned, "you do move rather rapidly, don't you?"

"I'm an aviator, you see," he answered.

Across the table Christine was trying to be gracious and graceful while she put up with Hickson, but she was feeling as any honest captain feels at having a prize cut out from under his very nose.

ALICE DUER MILLER

Mrs. Ussher seeing this, decided that such methods as Nancy's ought not to prevail; she seated herself on Max's other side, and instantly engaged in conversation.

"Don't you think my dear little Christine is an angel?" she said, without any encumbering subtlety.

"She certainly looks like one."

"Who looks like what?" asked Mrs. Almar, from his other side. She had had this sort of thing tried too often not to be on her guard.

Mrs. Ussher leant forward.

"Max was just saying that Christine looks like an angel."

Nancy looked at him and made a very slight grimace.

"Are you so awfully strong for angels?" she said. He laughed.

"I never met one before."

"You haven't met one tonight."

"You mean that you're not an angel, Mrs. Almar?"

"I? Oh, I'm well and favorably known as the wickedest woman in New York. I meant that Miss Fenimer is not an angel."

"You don't like her?"

"How you jump at conclusions! To say she isn't an angel, doesn't mean dislike. As a matter of fact, I am eager to secure her as my sister-in-law."

Riatt glanced at Hickson and was aware of the faintest possible pang. What qualities, he wondered, had a man like that.

"Oh," he said, "is she engaged to your brother?"

"Certainly not," answered Mrs. Almar. "But it is fairly well understood by every one except my brother, that if she doesn't find anything better within the next few years she will put up with him."

At this a slight feeling of disgust for both ladies took possession of Riatt.

"I see," he said rather coldly, and turned to Mrs. Ussher, but Nancy was not so easily disposed of.

"You mean," she went on, "that you see it is my duty as a sister to prevent anything else turning up. Suppose, for example, that a handsome, rich, attractive young man should suddenly appear upon the scene and show an interest in the angelic Christine." (By this time Riatt had turned again to her, and she looked straight into his eyes as she ran through her list of adjectives.) "Don't you think it would be my duty to distract his attention—to go almost any length to distract his attention?"

"However personally disagreeable to you the process might be?"

"Probably if he were as I described him, the process would not be so disagreeable."

He smiled. There was no denying he found her amusing.

In the meantime, the couple across the table had reached a somewhat similar point.

Hickson had said as they sat down:

"Well, and what do you think of this new fellow?"

Christine's natural irritation appeared in her answer.

"I have hardly had an opportunity of judging," she answered, "but, watching your sister's attentions to him, I would say he must be extremely attractive."

Hickson looked a little dashed.

"Oh," he said, "Nancy does not mean anything when she goes on like that."

The only effect of this speech was to depress further Miss Fenimer's estimate of her companion's intelligence, for in her opinion Nancy's whole life was one long black intention. Feeling this, Ned went on:

"As a matter of fact, one reason why she's so nice to him is to keep him away from you and give me a chance."

"Not very flattering to you, is it?"

"What do you mean?"

"The assumption that the only way to make a woman take an interest in you is to prevent her speaking to any other man."

"Oh, I didn't mean that—" Hickson began, but she interrupted him.

"That, if anything, Ned." And she turned to Wickham, who sat on her other side.

Wickham was waiting for a little notice and began instantly.

"I have been taking the liberty of looking at your pearls, Miss Fenimer, and indulging in such an interesting speculation. Here on the one hand, you are wearing round your throat the equivalent of life, health and virtue for half a hundred working girls, as young, as human, as yourself. Are we to say this is wrong? Are we to say that beautiful jewels worn by beautiful women are a crime against society—"

"One moment, Mr. Wickham," she said. "My pearls are imitation and cost eight dollars and fifty cents without the clasp. But," she added cruelly, seeing his face fall, "you can say that same thing to your friend Mrs. Almar, because hers are not artificial, though I have heard her assert sometimes that they are," and turning back to Hickson, who

ALICE DUER MILLER

was laboriously trying to carry on a conversation with his host, she interrupted ruthlessly to say, hardly lowering her voice:

"Why in the world, Ned, did Nancy bring this Wickham man here? He's perfectly impossible."

"Nancy didn't bring him," answered her brother innocently. "I motored out with her myself."

"She said she wouldn't come unless he were asked. Still I know the answer. Nancy has always had a weakness for blond boys, and last week she was crazy about this one. Now she has turned against him, she wants to foist him off on us, but I for one don't intend to help her out—"

By this time Wickham, aware that he had been rebuffed, had found an explanation for it. The girl was annoyed at having been forced to admit her pearls were imitation. He decided to put everything right.

"Miss Fenimer," he said, and she turned her head perhaps half an inch in his direction, "I think you misunderstood me just now. My standards are probably different from those of the men you are accustomed to. To me the fact that your pearls are not real is an added beauty. I'm glad they're not—"

"Thank you," said Christine, "but I'm not." And this time he understood that he had lost her for good.

After dinner, Mrs. Almar, knowing that her innings were over, very effectively prevented Christine having hers, by insisting on playing bridge. She had an excellent head for cards, and always needed money. Christine allowed herself to be drawn in, supposing that Riatt would be one of the players, and found herself seated opposite to Hickson and next to Jack Ussher.

Wickham, feeling very much left out and desirous of showing how well accustomed he was to the casual manners of polite society, consoled himself with an evening paper. Laura Ussher led Riatt to a comfortable corner out of earshot of the bridge-table.

"Now do tell me, Max," she said, "what you think of them all."

"I think, my dear Laura," he answered, "that they are a very playful band of cut-throats, and next time you ask me to stay, I hope you and Jack will be entirely alone."

THE SERVANTS IN A HOUSEHOLD like the Usshers' were subjected to almost every strain, except that of early rising. No one dreamed of coming down stairs before eleven, and most people not until lunch time.

The next morning Riatt was among the first—that is to say he was up early enough not to be able to escape a tour of inspection of the place under the guidance of his host. He had seen the stables and the new garage, and the sheet of snow beneath which lay the garden, and the other totally different sheet of snow beneath which was the soil in which Ussher intended next summer to plant a rose garden. He had gone over, tree by tree, the plantation of firs, and had noted how the tips of some were injured, and had given his opinion as to whether or not it were likely that deer had stolen down from the wild country near at hand and nibbled the young firs in the night.

"It's perfectly possible," said Ussher. "I have five hundred acres myself, and then the Club owns a huge tract, and then there's some state land. You see we have hardly any neighbors except the Fenimers and they're eight or nine miles away."

"They live here?"

"In summer—and then only when Fred Fenimer is in funds, and that's not often. A precarious sort of existence, his—gambling in mining stocks, almost always in wrong. Hard on the daughter—wish some nice fellow would come along and marry her."

"He probably will," answered Riatt rather coldly. "It's beginning to snow again."

Ussher had just had his pond swept so that his guests could skate, and now couldn't imagine what he should provide for them for the afternoon, so that his thoughts were instantly and completely turned from Christine's problems to his own.

At the house they found every one waiting for lunch; Mrs. Almar and Christine chattering together on a window-seat as if they were the most intimate allies; Hickson reading his fourth morning paper, and Mrs. Ussher paying the profoundest attention to something Wickham was saying. She had suddenly wakened to the fact that he was having a wretched time and that he was after all her guest. But he interpreted her actions differently, and supposing that he was at last being appreciated, he had launched fearlessly forth upon the conversational sea. It was this spectacle that had drawn Christine and Nancy together, in their whisperings and giggles in the window.

"This perhaps will illustrate my meaning," he was saying rather loudly: "this is the difference in our outlook on life. If you say 'she dresses well,' you intend a compliment, but to me it is just the reverse.

The idea is repellent to me that a woman wastes time, thought, money on her vanity, on decking her body—"

"One on you, my dear," whispered Christine.

"Isn't he tiresome?" answered Nancy, shutting her eyes.

"I thought he was your selection."

"Nobody's infallible, my dear. Besides, I telegraphed him not to accept the invitation, but he says he never got my message."

"Why does he think you sent it?"

"Because I couldn't trust myself—"

They grinned at each other.

With the entrance of Riatt and Ussher they went in to lunch, and there manoeuvering for places for the afternoon immediately began.

Hickson supposed that by starting early he could secure Christine's company. So he at once asked her what she was going to do, and before she had time to answer he had suggested that she skate, take a walk, or go sleighing with him. Ussher explained that the skating was spoiled, and Christine under cover of this diversion managed to avoid committing herself.

As a matter of fact her afternoon was arranged. She had told Laura Ussher a pathetic story of having to go over to her father's house, and look up an old fur coat of his which had been left behind when the house was shut for the winter. Mr. Fenimer was known to be rather an irritable parent where questions of his own comfort were concerned; it was not impossible that he would make himself disagreeable if his orders were not carried out. Laura did not inquire very closely, but she agreed that the best way for Christine to traverse the distance would be for Riatt to drive her over in the cutter. Riatt sat next to Laura at luncheon, and she put it to him, when the general conversation was loudest.

"Would you mind awfully driving poor little Christine over to her own place to get something or other for that horrid father of hers?"

Of course Riatt didn't say he did mind; as a matter of fact he didn't. He might even have enjoyed the prospect, if it hadn't been for the slight hint of compulsion about it.

"It's snowing, you know," he said.

"It doesn't amount to anything," answered his cousin. "But surely, Max, you're not afraid of a little snow, if she isn't!"

"Anything to oblige you, Laura," he said.

She did not quite like his tone, but felt she might safely leave the rest to Christine.

Mrs. Almar, unaware of these plots, settled down as soon as the meal was over, on a comfortable sofa large enough for two, with a box of cigarettes at her side and a current magazine that contained a new article on flying. The bird-like objects in the huge page of cloudy sky at once caught Max's eye. He came and bent over it and her, with his hands in his pockets. Still absorbed in it, she half-unconsciously swept aside her skirts, and he sat down beside her. She murmured a question— it was only about planes, and he answered it. Their heads were close together when Christine came down in her dark furs ready to go. The bells of Jack Ussher's fastest trotter were already to be heard tinkling at the door.

"Are you ready, Max?" said Laura, rather sharply.

"Laura expects every man to do his duty," murmured Nancy, without looking up.

Riatt expressed himself as entirely ready. Ussher lent him a fur cap and heavy gloves, warned him about the charmingly uncertain character of the horse; he and Christine were tucked into the sleigh, and they were off.

The snow, as Laura had said, did not seem to amount to much, the wind was behind them, the horse fast, the roads well packed. Riatt glanced down at his lovely companion, and felt his spirits rising. He smiled at her and she smiled back.

"I do hope you really feel like that," she said, "not sorry, I mean, to go on this expedition. Because it was extremely wicked of me to forget my father's coat, and this was obviously the occasion to make amends, but there was no one to take me—"

"No one to take you?"

"Oh, I suppose one of the grooms might have driven me over, but I should have hated that. There was no one else. Jack is much too selfish, and I wouldn't have gone with that Wickham person for anything in the world, even if he had ever driven a sleigh, which I am sure he hasn't."

"And how about Mr. Hickson?" Riatt asked. "Wasn't he a possibility?"

"What has Nancy Almar told you about her brother and me?"

"Nothing but what he told me himself in every look and word—that he loves you."

Christine sighed.

He smiled at her.

"And you're glad of it," he said.

"You mean I care for him?"

"I don't know anything about that, but you're glad he cares for you."

"You're utterly mistaken."

"How would you feel if another woman came and took him away from you tomorrow?"

"Took him away from me?" cried Christine, in a tone of surprise that made Riatt laugh aloud.

"That's the wonderful thing about the so-called weaker sex," he said. "Saying 'no' seems to have no terrors to them at all. The timidest girl will refuse a man with no more trouble and anxiety than she would expend on refusing a dinner invitation; whereas men, with all their vaunted courage, are absolutely at the mercy of a determined woman. I have a friend who has just married a girl—whom he three times explicitly refused—only because she asked him to."

Miss Fenimer looked at him thoughtfully.

"Surely you exaggerate," she said.

He shook his head sadly.

"I wish I did," he returned, "but I assure you that is the great secret— that any man would rather marry any woman than refuse her to her face. You see, no graceful way for a man to say 'no' has ever been discovered."

"Why, you poor defenseless creatures!" said Christine. "I'll teach you some ways immediately. I couldn't bear to think of your going about a prey to the first woman who proposed to you. Let us begin our lessons immediately. Have I your attention?"

"Completely."

"Let me see. In the first place there are several general types of proposal. There is the calmly rational, the passionate whirlwind, the dangerously controlled, or volcano under a sheet of ice—" she broke off. "I don't know how women do it," she said. "I only know about men."

He smiled, "But you admit to knowing all about them, I gather?"

It would have been folly to deny it.

"And then there's the meltingly pathetic," she went on. "I imagine that's what women attempt oftenest. Let us begin with that. Now you are to suppose that I, with tears streaming down my face, have just confessed that I have always looked up to you as a sort of god, that I hardly dare—"

"Wait, wait!" cried Riatt. "This is by far the most interesting part of the lesson, and you go so fast. I have no imagination. I don't know how it would be, you must say all those things."

"Do I have to cry?" said Christine.

Riatt debated the point.

"No," he answered at length, "I can imagine the tears, but everything else you must act out. Particularly that part about my seeming like a god to you."

"But how in the world can I teach you what to do, if I have to act a part myself?"

"Well, before we begin, just give me a sketch of what I ought to do."

"You must be very cold and firm, and explain to me that though my mistake is natural, you are really not a god at all; and then that gives you an excuse to talk a great deal about yourself, and tell how wicked and human and splendid you are, and that you are not worthy of a simple, good girl like myself, and how you don't love me anyhow. And then the essential thing is to go away quickly, and end the interview before I have a chance to begin all over again."

He looked doubtfully at the snow.

"Must I get out and walk home?" he asked.

"No," she said. "I think that's too complicated. We might try an easier one to begin. Suppose we do the calmly rational first. I explain to you that I have watched you from boyhood, and have come to the conclusion that our tastes, our intellects, our—"

"Oh, no," said Riatt, "there's really no use in going on with that. Even I should have no difficulty with any lady who approached me in that way. But there was one of the others that sounded rather promising and difficult. How about the passionate whirlwind? I say to try that next."

To her surprise, Christine found herself coloring a little.

"Ah," she said, laying her hand on her lips and shaking her head, "that's very difficult, because you see, it really can't be imitated—"

"Can't be imitated!" cried Max. "Why, what sort of a teacher are you? I believe you don't know your job. You are the sort of teacher who would tell an arithmetic class that long division could not be imitated. I believe the trouble with you is that you don't understand the passionate whirlwind yourself. I believe you're a fraud, and I shall have your license to teach taken away from you. Can't be imitated! Well, let me see you try, at least."

Christine felt that he had the better of her, but she said firmly:

"Are you teaching this subject, or am I?"

"Certainly you can't think *you* are. But if you say so, I'll have a try."

Not sorry to create a diversion, Christine looked about her, and was more diverted from the subject in hand than she had expected to be.

They were on the wrong road. What with the snow and the fact that she had been so busy talking that she really had no idea how far they had been, it took her a moment to orient herself anew. She told him with a conscience-struck look.

"And you," said Riatt, "who do not even know the road to your own house, were volunteering to pilot me through an emotional crisis."

Even a suggestion of adverse criticism was unpleasant to Miss Fenimer. She was not accustomed to it; and she answered with some sharpness:

"Yes, but the road is real, whereas I understand your embarrassment through the attentions of ladies is purely fictitious."

Riatt wondered how fictitious, but he turned the cutter about in obedience to her commands. The horse started forward even more gaily, under the impression that he was going home. But for the drivers, the change was not so agreeable. A high wind had come up, the snow was falling faster, and the light of the winter afternoon, already beginning to fade, was obscured by high, dark, silver-edged banks of clouds.

"Upon my word," said Riatt, "I think we had better go back."

"It's only a little way from here," Christine answered, trying hard to think how far it really was. She did want to get her father's coat, but she was not indifferent to the triumph of making Riatt late for dinner, and leaving Nancy Almar throughout the afternoon with no companion but Wickham or Jack Ussher.

The wind cut their faces, the horse pulled and pranced, the gaiety had gone out of their little expedition. They drove on a mile or so, and then Riatt stopped the horse.

"We've got to go back, Miss Fenimer," he said firmly.

"Oh, please not, Mr. Riatt; we are almost there, and," she added with a fine sense of filial obligation, "I really feel I must do as my father asked me."

Riatt felt inclined to point out that she, with her muff held up to her face, was not making the greatest sacrifice to the ideal of duty.

"Have you any very clear idea where your house is?" he asked. His tone was not flattering, and Christine was quick to feel it.

"Do I know where I live five months of the year?" she returned. "Of course I do. It's just over this next hill."

The afternoon was turning out so perversely that she would hardly have been surprised to find that the house had disappeared from its accustomed place. But as they came over the crest, there it was, in a hollow between two hills, looking as summer houses do in winter, like a forlorn toy left out in the snow.

"But it's shut up," said Riatt. "There's no one in it."

"I have the keys to the back door."

He touched the horse for the first time with the whip, and they went jingling down the slope, in between the almost completely buried gateposts, and drew up before the kitchen door.

Miss Fenimer kicked her feet free from the rugs, jumped out, and from the recesses of her muff produced a key which she inserted in the lock.

"Now you won't be long, will you?" said Riatt, with more of command than persuasion in his tone.

It was a principle of life on the part of Christine that she never allowed any man to bully her; or perhaps, it would be more nearly just to say that she never intended to allow any man to do so until she herself became persuaded that he could, and with this object she always made the process look as difficult and dangerous as possible at the very beginning.

She looked back at him and smiled with irritating calm.

"I shall be just as long as is necessary," she replied, and so saying, she turned, or rather attempted to turn, the key.

But disuse, or cold, or her own lack of strength prevented and she was presently reduced to asking Riatt to help her. He did not volunteer his assistance. She had definitely and directly to ask for it. Then he was friendliness itself.

"Just stand by the horse's head, will you?" he said, and when he saw her stationed there, he sprang out, and with an almost insulting ease opened the door.

Just as he did so, however, a gust of wind, fiercer than any other, swept round the corner of the house and carried away Christine's hat. She made a quick gesture to catch it, and as she did so, struck the horse under the chin. The animal reared, and Christine jumped aside to avoid being struck by its hoofs; the next instant, it had thrown its head in the air, and started at full speed down the road, dragging the empty sleigh after it. Riatt, who had his back turned, did not see the beginning of the incident, but a cry from Christine soon roused his attention, and he started in pursuit, calling to the animal to stop, in the hope that the human voice might succeed when all other methods were quite obviously useless. But the horse, now thoroughly excited by the hanging reins, the bells, and the sense of its own power, went only faster and faster, and finally disappeared at full speed.

Riatt came slowly back; he was sinking in the snow to his waist at every step. Christine was watching him with some anxiety.

"Is there a telephone in the house?" he asked.

She shook her head.

"No, it's disconnected when we leave in the autumn."

There was a moment's silence, then she said questioningly: "What shall we do?"

"There's only one thing we can do," he returned; "go into the house and light a fire."

But Christine hesitated.

"I don't think it will be wise to waste time doing that," she said, "if you have to go back on foot to the Usshers'—"

"Go back on foot!" Riatt interrupted. "My dear Miss Fenimer, that is quite impossible. It must be every inch of ten miles, it's dark, a blizzard is blowing, I don't know the way, and we haven't passed a house."

"But, but," said she, "suppose they don't rescue us tonight?"

"They probably will tomorrow," answered Riatt, and he walked past her into the house.

II

Christine was glad to get out of the wind, but the damp chill of the deserted house was not much of an improvement. Ahead of her in the darkness, she could hear Riatt snapping electric switches which produced nothing.

"Isn't the light connected?" he called.

"I don't know."

"Aren't there lamps in the house?"

"I don't know."

"Where could I find some candles?"

"What a tiresome man!" she thought; and for the third time she answered: "I don't know."

A rather unappreciative grunt was his only reply, and then he called back: "You'd better stay where you are, till I find something to make a light."

She asked nothing better. She was oppressed with a sense of crisis. An inner voice seemed to be saying, in parody of Charles Francis Adams's historic words: "I need hardly point out to your ladyship that this means marriage."

She had thought, lightly enough, that everything was settled the evening before on the stairs when she had made up her mind that he would do. But with all her belief in herself, she was not unaware even then that unforeseen obstacles might arise. He might be secretly engaged for all she knew to the contrary. But now she felt quite sure of him. With Fate playing into her hands like this—with romance and adventure and the possibilities of an uninterrupted tête-à-tête, she knew she could have him if she wanted him. And the point was that she did. At least she supposed she did. She felt as many a young man feels when he lands his first job—triumphant, but conscious of lost freedoms.

Marriage, she knew, was the only possible solution of her problems. Her life with her father was barely possible. As a matter of fact they were but rarely together. The tiny apartment in New York did not attract Fred Fenimer as a winter residence, when he had an opportunity of going to Aiken or Florida or California at the expense of some more fortunate friend. In summer it was much the same. "My dear," he would say to his daughter, "I really can't afford to open the house this summer." And Christine would coldly acquiesce, knowing that this statement only meant that he had received an invitation that he preferred to a quiet summer with her.

Sometimes throughout the whole season father and daughter would only meet by chance on some unexpected visit, or coming into a harbor on different yachts.

"Isn't that the *Sea-Mew's* flag?" Christine would say languidly. "I rather think my father is on board."

And then, perhaps, some amiable hostess in need of an extra man would send the launch to the *Sea-Mew* to bring Mr. Fenimer back to dine; and he would come on board, very civil, very neat, very punctilious on matters of yachting etiquette; and he and Christine having exchanged greeting, would find that they had really nothing whatsoever to say to each other.

Their only vital topic of conversation was money, and as this was always disagreeable, both of them instinctively tried to avoid it. Whenever Fenimer had money, he either speculated with it, or immediately spent it on himself. So that he was always able to say with perfect truth, whenever his daughter asked for it, that he had none. The result of this was that she had easily drifted into the simple custom of running up bills for whatever she needed, and allowing the tradesmen to fight it out with her father.

Such a system does not tend to economy. Christine's idea of what was necessary, derived from the extravagant friends who offered her the most opportunity for amusing herself, enlarged year by year. Besides, she asked herself, why should she deny herself, in order that her father might lose more money in copper stocks?

Sometimes during one of their casual meetings, he would say to her under his breath: "Good Heavens, girl, do you know, I've just had a bill of almost three thousand dollars from your infernal dressmaker? How can I stop your running up such bills?" And she would answer coolly: "By paying them every year or so."

She knew—she had always known since she was a little girl—that from this situation, only marriage could rescue her, and from the worse situation that would follow her father's death; for she suspected that he was deeply in debt. Not having been brought up in a sentimental school she was prepared to do her share in arranging such a marriage. In the world in which she lived, competition was severe. Already she had seen a possible husband carried off under her nose by a little school-room mouse who had had the aid of an efficient mother.

But now for the first time in her life, she saw that the game was in her own hands. She had only to do the right thing—only perhaps to avoid doing the wrong one—and her future was safe.

She heard Riatt calling and she followed him into the laundry, where he had collected some candles: he was much engaged in lighting a fire in the stove.

"But wouldn't the kitchen range be better?" she asked.

"No water turned on," he answered.

To her this answer was utterly unintelligible. What, she wondered, was the connection between fire and water. But, rather characteristically, she was disinclined to ask. She walked to the sink, however, and turned the tap; a long husky cough came from it, but no water.

After this burst of energy she sank into a chair, amused to watch his arrangements. Thoroughly idle people—and there is not much question that Miss Fenimer was idle—learn a variety of methods for keeping other people at work, and probably the most effective of these is flattery. Christine may have been ignorant of the feminine arts of cooking and fire-making; but of the super-feminine art of flattery she was a thorough mistress.

Now as Riatt finished building his fire, and began to bring in buckets of snow to supply their need of water, the gentle flow of her flattery soothed him as the sound of a hidden brook in the leafy month of June. Nor, strangely enough, did the fact that he dimly apprehended its purpose in the least interfere with his enjoyment.

"If ever I'm thrown away on a desert island, I speak to be thrown away with you," she said. "There isn't another man of my acquaintance who could bring order out of these primitive conditions."

He laughed. "Well, you know," he said, "this isn't really what you'd call primitive. I was snowed up in Alaska once."

"Alaska! You've been snowed up in Alaska?" she echoed in the tone of a child who says: was it a *black* bear?

Oh, yes, it lightened his toil. Nevertheless, he asked for her assistance in trying to find something to eat. She knew no more about the kitchen than he did, but she advanced toward a door and opened it gingerly between her thumb and forefinger. It was the kitchen closet. She opened a tin box.

"There is something here that looks like gravel," she called. He rushed to her side. It was cereal. He found other supplies, too, a little salt, sugar, coffee, and a jar of bacon.

"How clever of you to know what they all are," she murmured, and he felt as if he had invented them out of thin air, like an Eastern magician.

He carried them back to the kitchen. "I wonder if you'd get the coffee grinder," he said.

She hadn't the faintest idea what a coffee grinder looked like, but she went away to find it, and came back presently with an object strange enough to serve any purpose.

"Is this it?" she asked.

"That's a meat chopper," he answered, and then laughed. "You're not a very good housekeeper, are you?"

"Of course not," she said. "Did you ever know an agreeable woman who was? Good housekeepers are always bores, because they can never for an instant get their minds off the most tiresome things in the world like bills, and how the servants are behaving. All clever women are bad housekeepers, and so they always find some one like you to take care of them."

He was putting the cereal to boil, and answered only after a second. "Perhaps you'll think me old-fashioned, but I cannot help respecting the art of housekeeping."

"Oh, so do I in its place," replied Miss Fenimer. "My maid does the whole thing capitally. But let me give you a test. Think of the very best housekeeper you ever met. Would you like to have her here instead of me? You may be quite candid."

Riatt stopped and considered an instant with his head on one side. "She'd make me awfully comfortable," he said.

Miss Fenimer nodded, as much as to say: yes, but even so—

"No," he said at length, as if the decision had been close. "No, after all I would rather do the work and have you. But it isn't because you are a poor housekeeper that I prefer you. It's because—"

Compliments upon her, charms were platitudes to Christine, and she cut him short. "Yes, it is. It's because I'm so detached, and don't interfere, and let you do things your own way, and think you so wonderful to be able to do them at all. Now if I knew how to do them, too, I should be criticizing and suggesting all the time, and you'd have no peace. You like me for *being a poor housekeeper*."

He smiled. "On that ground I ought to like you very much then," he answered.

"Perhaps you do," she said cheerfully. "Anyhow I'm sure you like me better than that other girl you were thinking of—that good housekeeper. Who is she?"

"I like her quite a lot."

"I see—you think she'd make a good wife."

"I think she'd make a good wife to any man who was fortunate enough—"

"Oh, what a dreadful way to talk of the poor girl!"

"On the contrary, I admire her extremely."

"I believe you are engaged to her."

"Not as much as you are to Hickson."

Christine laughed. "From the way you describe her," she said, "I believe she'd make a perfect wife for Ned."

"Oh, she's much too good for him."

"Thank you. You seem to think I'll do nicely for him."

"Ah, but she's much better than you are."

"And yet you said you'd rather have me here than her."

He smiled. "I think," he said, and Christine rather waited for his next words, "I think I shall go down and see if I can't get the furnace going."

Nevertheless, she said to herself when he was gone, "I should not feel at all easy about him, if I were the other girl."

She knew there was no prospect of their being rescued that night. When the sleigh arrived at the Usshers', if it ever did arrive, its empty shattered condition would suggest an accident. The Usshers were at that moment probably searching for them in ditches, and hedges. The marks of the sleigh would be quickly obliterated by the storm. No, she thought comfortably, there was no escape from the fact that their situation was compromising. The only question was how could the matter be most tactfully called to his attention. At the moment he seemed happily unaware that such things as the proprieties existed.

At this his head appeared at the head of the cellar stairs.

"Watch the cereal, please," he said, "and see that it doesn't burn."

"Like King Alfred?"

"Not too much like him, please, for that pitiful little dab of food is about all we have to eat."

When he was gone Christine advanced toward the stove and looked at the cereal—looked at it closely, but it seemed to her to be but little benefited by her attention. Presently she discovered on a shelf beside the laundry clock a pinkish purple paper novel, called: "The Crime of the Season." Its cover depicted a man in a check suit and side-whiskers looking on in astonishment at the removal of a drowned lady in full evening dress from a very minute pond. Christine opened it, and was so fortunate as to come full upon the crime. She became as completely absorbed in it as the laundress had been before her.

She was recalled to the more sordid but less criminal surroundings of real life by a strong pungent smell. She sniffed, and then her heart suddenly sank as she realized that the cereal was burning. She recognized a peculiarly disagreeable flavor about which she had often scolded the cook, thinking such carelessness on the part of one of her employees to be absolutely inexcusable.

She ran to the head of the cellar stairs. "Mr. Riatt!" she called.

He was now shaking down the furnace, and the noise completely drowned her voice. "Oh, dear, what a noisy man he is," she thought and when he had finished, she called again: "Mr. Riatt!"

This time he heard. "What is it?" he answered.

"Mr. Riatt, what shall I do? The cereal is burning terribly."

"I should think it was," he said. "I can smell it down here." He sprang up the stairs and snatched the pot from the stove. "You must have stopped stirring it," he said.

"Oh, I didn't stir it!"

"What did you do?"

"You didn't tell me to stir it."

"I certainly did."

"No, you said just to watch it."

Riatt looked at her. "Well," he said, "I've heard of glances cutting like a knife, but never stirring like a spoon. If I were a really just man," he went on, "I'd make you eat that burnt mess for your supper, but I'm so absurdly indulgent that I'll share some of my bacon and biscuits with you."

His tone as well as his words were irritating to one not used to criticism in any form.

"I don't care for that sort of joke," she said.

"I wasn't aware of having made a joke."

"I mean your attitude as if I were a child that had been naughty."

"It wouldn't be so bad if you were a child."

"You consider me to blame because that wretched cereal chose to burn?"

"Emphatically I do."

"How perfectly preposterous," said Christine, and a sense of bitter injustice seethed within her. "Why in the world should *I* be expected to know how to cook?"

"I'm a little too busy at the moment to explain it to you," Riatt answered, "but I promise to take it up with you at a later date."

There was something that sounded almost like a threat in this. She turned away, and walking to the window stood staring out into the darkness. He was really quite a disagreeable young man, she thought. How true it was, that you couldn't tell what people were like when everything was going smoothly. She wondered if he would always be like that—trying to keep one up to one's duty and making one feel stupid and ignorant about the merest trifles.

"Well, this rich meal is ready," he said presently.

She turned around. The table was set—she couldn't help wondering where he had found the kitchen knives and forks—the bacon was sizzling, the tin of biscuits open, and the coffee bubbling and gurgling in its glass retort.

She sat down and began to eat in silence, but as she did so, she studied him furtively. She was used to many different kinds of masculine bad temper; her father's irritability whenever anything affected his personal comfort: and from other men all forms of jealousy and hurt feelings. But this stern indifference to her as a human being was something a little different. She decided on her method.

"Oh, dear," she said, "this meal couldn't be much drearier if we were married, could it?"

"Except," he returned, unsmilingly, "that then it would be one of a long series."

"Not as far as I'm concerned," she answered. "I should leave you on account of your bad temper."

"If I hadn't first left you on account of—"

"Of burning the cereal?"

"Of being so infernally irresponsible about it."

"Oh, that's the trouble, is it?" she said. "That I did not seem to care? Well, I assure you that I don't like burnt food any better than you do, but I have some self-control. I wouldn't spoil a whole evening just because—" A sudden inspiration came to her. Her voice failed her, and she hid her face in her pocket handkerchief.

Riatt leant back in his chair and looked at her, looked at least at the back of her long neck, and the twist of her golden hair and the occasional heave of her shoulders.

The strange and the humiliating thing was that she had just as much effect upon him when he quite obviously knew that she was insincere.

"Why," he said gently, "are you crying? Or perhaps I ought to say, why are you pretending to cry?"

She paid no attention to the latter part of his question.

"You're so unkind," she said, careful not to overdo a sob. "You don't seem to understand what a terrible situation this is for me."

"In what way is it terrible?"

"Don't you know that a story like this clings to a girl as long as she lives? That among the people I know there will always be gossip—"

"You're not serious?"

She nodded, still behind her handkerchief, "Yes, I am. This will be something I shall have to live down, as much as you would if you had robbed a bank."

She now raised her head, and wiping her eyes hard enough to make them a little red, she glanced at him.

Really she thought it would save a great deal of time and trouble, if he could just see the thing clearly and ask her to marry him now.

But apparently his mind did not work so quickly.

"Who will repeat it?" he said. "Not the Usshers—"

"Nancy Almar won't let it pass. She'll have found the evening dull without you, and she'll feel she has a right to compensation. And that worm, Wickham; it will be his favorite anecdote for the rest of his life. I was horrible to him last night at dinner."

"Sorry you were?"

"Not a bit. I'd do it again, but I may as well face the fact that he won't be eager to conceal his own social triumphs for the sake of my good name. Can't you hear him, 'Curious thing happened the other day—at my friends the Usshers'. Know them? A lovely country place—'—"

"I'm awfully sorry," he said. "What a bore! Is there anything I could do—"

"Well, there is one thing."

He looked up quickly. If ever terror flashed in a man's eyes, she saw it then in his. Her heart sank, but her mind worked none the less well.

"It's this," she went on smoothly. "There's a lodge, a sort of tool-house, only about half a mile down the road. Couldn't you take a lantern, couldn't you possibly spend the night there?"

"It isn't by any chance," he said, "that you're afraid of having me here?"

"Oh, no, not you," she answered. "No, I should feel much safer with you here than there." (If he went her case was ruined, and she was now actually afraid perhaps he would go.) "I should be terrified in this great place all by myself. Still, I think you ought to go. It's not so very far. You go down the road a little way and then turn to the right through the woods. I think you'll find it. The roof used to leak a little, but I dare say you won't mind that. There isn't any fireplace, but you could take lots of blankets—"

"I tell you what I'll do," he said. "No one will come to rescue us tonight. I'll sleep here tonight, and tomorrow as soon as it's light, I'll go to this cottage, and when they come, you can tell them any story you please. Will that do?"

It did perfectly. "Oh, thank you," she said. "How kind you are! And you do forgive me, don't you?"

"About the cereal? Oh, yes, on one condition."

"What is that?" She was still meltingly sweet.

"That you wash these dishes."

She felt inclined to box his ears. Had he seen through her all the time?

"I never washed a dish in my life," she observed thoughtfully.

"Have you ever done anything useful?"

She reflected, and after some thought she replied, not boastfully, but as one who states an indisputable fact: "Never."

He folded his arms, leant against the wall and looked down upon her. "I wish," he said, "if it isn't too much trouble that you would give me a detailed account of one of your average days."

"You talk," said she, "as if you were studying the manners and customs of savages."

"Let us say of an unknown tribe."

She leant back in her chair and stretched her arms over her head. "Well, let me see," she said. "I wake up about nine or a little after if I haven't been up all night, and I ring for my maid. And about eleven—"

"Don't skip, please. You ring for your maid. What does she do for you?"

Imagine any one's not knowing! Miss Fenimer marveled. "Why, she draws my bath and puts out my things, and while I'm taking my bath, she straightens the room and lights the fire, if it's cold, and brings in my breakfast-tray and my letters. And by half-past ten, I'm finally dressed if no one has come in to delay me, only some one always has. Last winter my time was immensely occupied by two friends of mine who had both fallen in love with the same man—one of them was married to him—and they used to come every day and confide in me. You have no idea how amusing it was. He behaved shockingly, but I couldn't help feeling a little sorry for him. They were both such determined women. Finally I went to him, and told him how it was I knew so much about his affairs, and said I thought he ought to try and make up his mind which of them he really did care for. And what do you think he said? That he had always been in love with me." She laughed. "How absurdly things happen, don't they?"

"Good Heavens!" said Riatt.

"But even at the worst, I'm generally out by noon, and get a walk. I'm rather dependent on exercise, and then I lunch with some one or other—"

"Men or women?"

"Either or both. And then after lunch I drive with some one, or go to see pictures or hear music, and then I like to be at home by tea time, because that's, of course, the hour every one counts on finding you; and then there's dressing and going out to dinner, and very often something afterwards."

"Good Lord," said Riatt again, and after a moment he added: "And does that life amuse you?"

"No, but it doesn't bore me as much as doing things that are more trouble."

"What sort of things?"

"Oh, being on committees that you don't really take any interest in." She rather enjoyed his amazement.

"Now tell me one thing more," he said. "What would you do if you had to earn your living?"

The true answer was that she would marry Edward Hickson, but, though heretofore she had been fairly candid, she thought on this point a little dissembling was permissible. "I should starve, I suppose," she returned gaily.

"And suppose you fell in love with a poor man?"

She grew grave at once. "Oh, that's a dreadful thing to happen to one," she said. "I've had two friends who did that." She almost shuddered. "One actually married him."

"And what happened to her?"

Miss Fenimer shook her head. "I don't know. She's living in the suburbs somewhere. I haven't seen her for ages."

"And the other?"

"She was more practical. She married him to a rich widow ten years older than he was. That provided for him, you see, at least. But it turned out worse than the other case."

"How?"

"Why, he fell in love with this other woman—"

"His wife, you mean?"

"Yes. Imagine it! Men are so fickle."

"Do you know that you really shock me?"

"It's better to appreciate the way things are."

"It isn't the way things are among decent normal human beings."

She shrugged her shoulders. "Oh, I imagine it is," she said, "only they're not honest enough to admit it."

He continued to stare at her and, strangely enough, she had never seemed to him more beautiful.

"And do you mean to tell me," he said, "that people who have the standards that you describe will attach the slightest importance to an innocent little adventure like this of ours?"

"Of course. They are the very people who will."

"Nonsense."

"Yes, because they make a point of always believing the worst, or at least of pretending to."

"Why pretend?"

"Because it makes conversation so much more amusing. Sometimes," she added thoughtfully, "I have a terrible suspicion that there really isn't an atom of harm in any of them—that they all behave perfectly well, and just excite themselves by talking as if they didn't."

"And you call that suspicion terrible?"

"Well, it makes it all seem a little flat. But then sometimes," she went on brightly, "one does find out something absolutely hideous."

"See here," he said, "it's a crime for a girl of your age to talk like this. It's a silly habit. I don't believe you're like that at heart."

"You talk," said she, "like Edward Hickson."

"In some communities that would be thought a fighting word," he returned. "But you haven't yet answered my question. You've told me what your friends have done; but what would you do yourself, if you fell in love with a poor man?"

"In the first place, I never should. What makes a man attractive to me is power, preeminence, being bowed down to. If I lived in a military country, I'd love the greatest soldier; and if I lived in a savage country, I'd love the strongest warrior; but here today, the only form of power I see is money. It's what makes you able to have everything you want, and that's a man's greatest charm."

"And it seems to me that the most tied-down creatures I ever saw are the rich men I've met in the East."

She was honestly surprised. "Why, what is there they can't do?" she asked.

He smiled. "They can't do anything that might endanger their property rights," he answered, "and that seems to me to cut them off from most forms of human endeavor. But no matter about that. You say you would not be likely to fall in love with a poor man, but suppose you *did*. Perhaps it has happened already?"

Miss Fenimer looked thoughtful. "I was trying to think," she said. "Yes, there was a young artist two years ago that I was rather interested in. He was very nice looking, and Nancy Almar kept telling me how much he was in love with her."

"And that stimulated your interest?"

"Of course."

"Just for the sake of information," he said, "do you always want to take away any man who is safely devoted to another woman?"

Christine seemed resolved to be accurate. "It depends," she answered, "whether or not I have anything else to do, but of course the idea always pops into one's head: I wonder if I couldn't make him like me best."

"And do you always find you can?"

"Oh, there's no rule about it; only as a newcomer one has the advantage of novelty, and that's something."

"And what happened about this artist?"

Christine smiled reminiscently: "I found he wasn't really in love with Nancy at all: he just wanted to paint her portrait."

"I should think he would have wanted to paint yours."

"He did and gave it to me as a present, and then he behaved very badly." She sighed.

"What did he do?"

"Well," she hesitated. "He did not really want to give me the picture. He thought he wanted to keep it himself. It was much the best thing he ever did. I had to persuade him a good deal, and in persuading him, I may have given him the impression that I cared about him more than I really did. Anyhow, after I actually had the portrait hanging in my sitting-room, I told him I thought it was better for us not to meet any more. Some men would have been flattered to think I took them so seriously. But he was furious, and one day when I was out he sent for the portrait and cut it all to pieces. Wasn't that horrible? My pretty portrait!"

"Horrible!" said Riatt. "It seems to me the one spark of spirit the poor young man showed."

She glanced at him under her lashes. "What would you have done?"

"I'd take you out to the plains for a year or so, and let you find out a little about what life is like."

"I don't think it would be a success," she returned. "I don't profit by discipline, I'm afraid. But," she stood up, "I'm perfectly open minded. I'll make a beginning. I'll wash the dishes—just to please you."

He watched her go to the kitchen sink, and pour water from the steaming kettle into a dish pan, saw her turn up her lace-frilled cuffs, and begin with her long, slim, inefficient hands to take up the dirty plates. Suddenly, much to his surprise, he found he couldn't bear it, couldn't bear to see the lace fall down again and again, and her obvious shrinking from the task.

He crossed the room and took the plates from her, and then with a clean towel, he deliberately dried her hands, finger by finger, while she stood by like a docile child, looking up at him in wonder.

"Don't you want to reform me?" she asked plaintively.

"No," he answered shortly.

"Why not?"

"Because you would be too dangerous," he returned. "Now you have every charm except goodness. If you turned good and gentle you'd be supreme."

"I never thought goodness was a *charm*," she objected.

"And that's just what I hope you will never find out."

She laughed. "I don't believe there's much danger," she said. "I think I shall go on being wicked and mercenary and selfish to the day of my death, and probably getting everything I want."

"I hope not. I mean I hope you won't get what you want."

"Oh, why are you so unkind?"

"Because I shall want to use you as a terrible example to my grandchildren."

"Do you think you will remember me as long as that?"

"I feel no doubt about it."

She smiled. "It seems rather hard that I have to come to a bad end just to oblige your horrid little grandchildren," she said. "As a matter of fact, I shall probably run them down in my motor as they go to work with their little dinner-pails. And as I take their mangled forms to the hospital, I'll murmur: 'Riatt, Riatt, I think I once knew a half-hearted reformer of that name.'"

"You think you, too, will remember as long as that?"

"I have an excellent memory for trifles," she returned, and rose yawning. "And now I think I'll go to bed—unless there's anything more you want to know about our tribal customs. Are you going to write a nature book about us: 'Head-hunting Among the Idle Rich'?"

"'The Cannibals of the Atlantic Coast' is the title," he answered as he gave her a candle. "I'll leave your breakfast for you in the morning before I go. And by the way, if some one comes to rescue you, don't go off and leave me in the tool-house, will you?"

"Oh, I'm not really as bad as that."

He shook his head as if he didn't feel sure.

She went away well satisfied with her evening's work. There had been something extremely flattering in his mingled horror and amusement at her candid revelations. Holding up the candle she looked at her own image in her mirror. "I wonder," she thought, "if that young man knows what a dangerous frame of mind he's in?"

He had some suspicion, for as he dragged a mattress downstairs and laid it before the kitchen fire, he kept repeating to himself, as if in a last effort to rouse some moral enthusiasm: "What a band of cut-throats they are!"

Christine woke the next morning to find the sun shining on an unbroken sheet of snow. The storm had passed in the night. She dressed quickly and went down to find the kitchen empty, and the track of footsteps in the snow leading away in the direction of the tool-house. Her coffee was bubbling and slices of bacon neatly laid in the frying pan were ready for cooking. She thought he might have stayed and cooked it for her.

"No one will come as early as this," she thought, plaintively.

But hardly had she finished her simple meal, when the sound of sleigh bells reached her ears, and running to the window she saw that Ussher and Hickson in a two horse sleigh were driving down the slope.

A moment later they were in the kitchen. And after the minimum time had elapsed during which all three talked at once recounting their own individual anxieties, Ussher asked:

"Where's Max?"

Christine cast down her eyes with a sort of Paul-and-Virginia expression, as she answered: "Oh, he is sleeping in the tool-house!"

"Well, I call that damned nonsense," said Ussher. "Let a man freeze to death! Upon my word, Christine, I thought you had more sense." And he strode away to the back door. "Yes, here are his tracks, poor fellow." Ussher went out after him, and Hickson turned back.

"But *you* think I was right, don't you, Edward?" said Christine, for she had never failed to elicit commendation from Edward.

But now his brow was dark. "But, I say, Christine," he said, "there's one thing I don't understand. These tracks of his footsteps in the snow."

"He didn't fly, Ned, even if he is an aviator."

"Yes, but it didn't stop snowing until four o'clock this morning."

How irritating the weather always is, Christine thought. For though she was willing to use scandal as a weapon over Riatt, she was not sure that she wished to put it into Hickson's hands.

She thought hard, and then said brightly:

"Oh, perhaps he came back for his breakfast before I was up."

Hickson shook his head: "They only lead one way," he said.

In the face of the tactlessness of hard facts, Christine decided to create a diversion.

"I can't stand here gossiping about the conduct of an aviator," she said, "when there's so much to be done. Look at all these dirty plates. What ought to be done with them, Edward, dear?" she appealed to him as to a fountain of wisdom, and he did not fail her.

"They ought to be washed," he said. "Give me a towel. I'll do it." And he felt more than rewarded when, as she handed him a towel, her hand touched his.

The many duties of which she had just spoken seemed suddenly to have melted away, for she sat down quite idly and watched him.

"How well you do it, Edward," she said, not quite honestly, for she compared his slow gestures very unfavorably with Riatt's deft hands. "It's quite as if you had washed dishes all your life."

"Ah, Christine," he answered, looking at her sentimentally over a coffee-cup, "I shouldn't ask anything better than to wash your dishes for the rest of my life."

"Thank you, Edward, but I think I should ask something a good deal better," she answered.

It was on this scene that Ussher and Riatt entered, and the eyes of the latter twinkled.

"Engaged a kitchen-maid, I see," he said in a low tone to Christine.

"I think it's so good for people to do something useful now and then, don't you?"

"A form of education that you offer almost every one who comes near you."

Hickson did not hear everything, but he caught the idea, and said severely:

"I don't suppose any one would ask Miss Fenimer to wash dirty dishes."

Riatt laughed: "No one who had ever seen her try."

Ussher, who had been fuming in the background, now broke out:

"Upon my word, Christine, that tool-house was like a vault. It was madness to ask any one to spend the night in such a place."

"Did you spend the night in the tool-house?" said Hickson with unusual directness.

"There are worse places than the tool-house," said Riatt, as he and Ussher hurried down to the cellar to put out the furnace fire.

Hickson turned to Christine. "The fellow didn't answer me," he said.

"Perhaps he thought it was none of your business, Edward, my dear," she answered.

"Everything connected with you is my business," he returned.

"Oh, Edward, what a dreary outlook for me!"

"Christine, answer me. Did or did not this man make advances to you?"

"Edward, he did."

"What happened?"

"He gave me a long, tiresome, moral lecture and, judging by you, my dear, that is proof of affection."

"You're simply amusing yourself with me!"

"I'm not amusing myself very much, Edward, if that's any comfort."

"You drive me mad," he said and stamped away from her so hard, that Ussher came up from the cellar.

"What's Edward doing?" he said.

"He says he's going mad," returned Christine, "but I thought he was washing the dishes."

"There's no pleasing Edward," said Ussher. "He was in my room at six o'clock this morning trying to get me to start a rescuing party (and I needn't tell you, Christine, we none of us had much sleep last night), and now that he is here and finds you safe, he seems to be just as restless as ever." And Ussher returned to the cellar still grumbling.

"You know why I'm restless, Christine," Hickson said when they were again alone.

Christine seemed to wonder. "The artistic temperament is usually given as the explanation, but somehow, in your case, Edward—"

He came and stood directly in front of her.

"Christine, what did happen last night?"

Although not a muscle of Miss Fenimer's face moved, she knew very well that this was a turning-point. She had the choice between killing the scandal, or giving it such life and strength that nothing but her marriage with Riatt would ever allay it. She knew that a few sensible words would put Hickson straight, and Hickson would be a powerful ally. On the other hand, if he came back plainly weighted with a terrible doubt, no one would ask any further evidence. The question was, how much would Riatt feel the responsibility of such a situation. It was a fighting chance. Themistocles when he burnt his ships must have argued in very much the same way, but probably not so rapidly.

"There are some things, Edward," Christine said in a low shaken voice, "that I cannot discuss even with you."

Hickson turned away with a groan.

III

Christine had been right when she told Riatt that Nancy Almar would be resentful after a dull evening at the Usshers'.

The evening, as far as Nancy was concerned, had been very dull indeed. To be bored, in her creed, was a confession of complete failure; it indicated the most contemptible inefficiency, since she designed the whole fabric of her life with the unique object of keeping herself amused. Nothing bored her more than to have the general attention centered on some one else, as all that evening it had been focussed on the absent ones. Not only did she miss the excitement of her contest with Christine over the possession of Riatt, but she was positively wearied by the Usshers' anxiety, by her brother's agony of jealousy and fear, and by Wickham's continual effort to strike an original thought from the dramatic quality of the situation.

She was finally reduced to playing piquet with Wickham, and though she won a good deal of money from him—more, that is, than he could comfortably afford to lose—she still counted the evening a failure, bad in the present, and extremely menacing to the future. For with her habitual mental candor, she admitted that by this time Christine, if not actually frozen to death—which after all one could not exactly hope—had probably won the game. The chances were that Riatt was captured.

"What is the matter, Ned?" she said to her brother, as he fidgeted about the card-table, after a last futile expedition to the telephone. "Can't you decide whether you'd rather the lady of your love were dead or subjected for twenty-four hours to the fascinations of an irresistible young man?"

"What an interesting question that raises," observed Wickham, examining rather ruefully the three meager cards he had drawn. "A modern Lady-or-the-Tiger idea. I am not of a jealous temperament and should always prefer to see a woman happy with another man."

"And often do, I dare say," said Nancy. "I have a point of seven, and fourteen aces."

"I must own I can't see Riatt's irresistible quality," said Hickson irritably.

"Rich, nice-looking and has his wits about him," replied Mrs. Almar succinctly.

"About as good-looking as a fence-rail."

"And they say women are envious!" exclaimed his sister.

"Are you a feminist, Mrs. Almar?" inquired the irrepressible Wickham.

"No, just a female, Mr. Wickham."

"I never thought a big bony nose made a man a beauty," grumbled Hickson.

"Ah, how much wisdom there is in that reply of yours, Mrs. Almar," said Wickham. "Just a female. Your meaning is, if I interpret you rightly, that you are content with the duties and charms which Nature has bestowed upon your sex—"

"Until I can get something better," replied Nancy briskly, drawing the score toward her and beginning to add it up. "My idea is to let the other women do the fighting; if they win, I shall profit; if they lose, I'm no worse off. I believe I've rubiconed you again, Mr. Wickham."

"Well, I don't understand women's taste, anyhow," said Hickson.

"You never spoke a truer word than that, my dear," said Nancy. "Seventy-four fifty, I think that makes it, Mr. Wickham, subtracting the dollar and a half you made on the first game. Oh, yes, a check will do perfectly. I'm less likely to lose it."

"I never had a worse run of luck," observed Wickham with an attempt at indifference.

Mrs. Almar stood up yawning. "Doubtless you are on the brink of a great amorous triumph," she said languidly, and went off to bed.

Hickson did not attempt to sleep. He sat up for the remainder of the night, in the hope that some sudden call might come, and at six o'clock as Ussher had told Christine, he was ready for new efforts.

Rescued and rescuers reached the Usshers' house about half past ten the following morning. Nancy was not yet downstairs. Wickham had not been able to judge what was the correct note to strike in connection with the whole incident, and so did not dare to sound any. The arrival was comparatively simple. Mrs. Ussher received her beloved Christine with open arms; Riatt went noncommittally upstairs to take a bath; Hickson had decided, in spite of his depression of spirits, to try to make up a little of last night's lost sleep, when he received a summons from his sister. Her maid, a clever, sallow little Frenchwoman, came down with her hands in her apron pockets to say that Madame should like to speak to Monsieur at once.

He found Nancy still in bed; her little black head looking blacker than usual against the lace of the pillows and the coverlet and of her own bed-jacket. The only color about her was the yellow covered French novel she laid down as he entered, and the one enormous ruby on her fourth finger.

"And now, Ned, my dear," she said quite affectionately for her, "I hear you have brought the wanderers safely home. Tell me all about it."

Hickson, to whom this summons had not come as a surprise, had resolved that he would confide none of his anxieties to his sister but, alas, as well might a pane of glass resolve to be opaque to a ray of sunlight. Within ten minutes, Nancy knew not only all that he knew, but such additional deductions as her sharper wits enabled her to draw.

"I see," she murmured, as he finished. "The only positive fact that we have is that he did not leave the house until after five. How very interesting!"

"Very terrible," said Hickson.

"Terrible," exclaimed Nancy, with the most genuine surprise. "Not at all. From your point of view most encouraging. It can mean only one thing. The young man very prudently ran away."

Edward was really stirred to anger. "Nancy," he said, "how do you dare, even in fun—"

"Oh, my dear," answered his sister, as one wearied by all the folly in the world, "how can I be of any use to you if you will not open your eyes? He ran away. We don't know of course just from what; but we do know this: Max Riatt is the best match that has yet presented himself, and that Christine is the last girl in the world to ignore that simple fact. Come, Ned, even if you do love her, you may as well admit the girl is not a perfect fool. Fate, accident, or possibly her own clever manoeuvering put the game into her hands. The question is, how did she play it? I know what I'd have done, but I don't believe she would. I think she probably tried to make him believe that she was hopelessly compromised in the eyes of the world, and that there was no course open to an honorable man but to ask her to marry him."

"I can't imagine Christine playing such a part."

"I tell you, you never do the poor girl justice. If she did that—and the chances are she did—then his running away is most encouraging. It means, in your own delightful language, that he did not fall for it— did not want to run any risk of compromising her, if marriage was the consequence."

"But, Nancy, Christine almost admitted that—that he tried to make love to her."

"I can't see what that has to do with it, or what difference it makes," replied Mrs. Almar. "However, too much importance should not be attached to such admissions. I have sometimes made them myself when the facts did not bear me out. No woman likes to confess, especially to an old adorer like you, that she has spent so many hours alone with a man and he has not made love to her."

Hickson shook his head. "I'm not clever enough to be able to explain it," he said, "but I received the clearest impression from her that she had been through some painful experience."

"Good," said Nancy. "Do you know the most painful experience she could have been through?"

"No, what?"

"If he hadn't paid the slightest attention to her; and that, my dear brother, is what I am inclined to think took place. No, the game is still on; only now she'll have the Usshers to help her. This is no time for me to lie in bed."

Ned looked at her doubtfully. "I thought I'd try and sleep a little," he said.

"The best thing you can do," she returned. "Lucie! Lucie! Where are the bells in this house! What privations one suffers for staying away from home! Oh, yes, here it is," and she caught the atom of enamel and gold dangling at the head of her bed, and rang it without ceasing until the maid, who regarded her mistress with an admiration quite untinctured by affection, appeared silently at the doorway.

In an astonishingly short space of time, she was dressed and downstairs, presenting her usual sleek and polished appearance. Wickham was alone in the drawing-room, and a suggestion that they should have another game of piquet quickly drove him to the writing of some purely imaginary business letters.

The coast was thus clear, but Riatt was still absent.

Nancy's methods were nothing if not direct. She rang the bell and when the butler appeared she said:

"Where is Mr. Riatt?"

"In his room, madam."

"Dressing?"

"No, madam, he is dressed. Resting, I should say."

Nancy nodded her head once. "One moment," she said; and going to the writing table she sat down and wrote quickly:

ALICE DUER MILLER

"I should like five minutes' conversation with you. Strange to say my motive is altruistic—so altruistic that I feel I should sign myself 'Pro Bono Publico,' instead of Nancy Almar. There is no one down here in the drawing-room at the moment."

She put this in an envelope, sealed it with sealing wax (to the disgust of the butler who found it hard enough, as it was, to keep up with all that went on in the house) and told the man to send it at once to Mr. Riatt's room.

She did not have long to wait. Riatt, with all the satisfaction in his bearing of one who has just bathed, shaved and eaten, came down to her at once.

"Good morning, Pro Bono Publico," he said, just glancing about to be sure he was not overheard. "It was not necessary to put this interview on an altruistic basis. I should have been glad to come to it, even if it had been as a favor to you."

She looked at him with her hard, dark eyes. "Isn't that rather a reckless way for a man in your situation to talk?"

"I was not aware that I was in a situation."

This was exactly the expression that she had wanted from him. It seemed to come spontaneously, and could only mean that at least he was not newly engaged.

She relaxed the tension of her attitude. "Are you really under the impression that you're not?"

"I feel quite sure of it."

"You poor, dear, innocent creature."

"However," he went on, sitting down beside her on the wide, low sofa, "something tells me that I shall enjoy extremely having you tell me all about it."

Tucking one foot under her, as every girl is taught in the school-room it is most unladylike to do, she turned and faced him. "Mr. Riatt," she said, "when I was a child I used to let the mice out of the traps—not so much, I'm afraid, from tenderness for the mice, as from dislike of my natural enemy, the cook. Since then I have never been able to see a mouse in anybody's trap but my own, without a desire to release it."

"And I am the mouse?"

She nodded. "And in rather a dangerous sort of trap, too."

He smiled at the seriousness of her tone.

"Ah," said she, "the self-confidence which your smile betrays is one of the weaknesses by which nature has delivered your sex into the hands of mine. I would explain it to you at length, but the time is too short. The great offensive may begin at any moment. The Usshers have made up their minds that you are to marry Christine Fenimer. That was why you were asked here."

"Innocent Westerner as I am," he answered, "that idea—"

She interrupted him. "Yes, but don't you see it's entirely different now. Now they really have a sort of hold on you. I don't know what Christine's own attitude may be, but I can tell you this: her position was so difficult that she was on the point of engaging herself to Ned."

"Oh, come," said Riatt politely, "your brother is not so bad as you seem to think."

"He's not bad at all, poor dear. He's very good; but women do not fall in love with him. You, on the contrary, are rich and attractive. You'll just have to take my word for that," she added without a trace of coquetry. "And so—and so—and so, if I were you, my dear Cousin Max, I should give orders to have my bag packed at once, and take a very slow, tiresome train that leaves here at twelve-forty-something, and not even wait for the afternoon express."

There was that in her tone that would have made the blood of any man run cold with terror, but he managed a smile. "In my place you would run away?" he said.

She shook her head. "No, I wouldn't run away myself, but I advise you to. I shouldn't be in any danger. Being a mere woman, I can be cruel, cold and selfish when the occasion demands. But this is a situation that requires all the qualities a man doesn't possess."

"What do you mean?"

"Does your heart become harder when a pretty woman cries? Is your conscience unmoved by the responsibility of some one else's unhappiness? Can you be made love to without a haunting suspicion that you brought it on yourself?"

"Good heavens, no!" cried Riatt from the heart.

"Then, run while there's time."

As the ox fears the gad-fly and the elephant the mouse, so does the bravest of men fear the emotional entanglement of any making but his own. For an instant Riatt felt himself swept by the frankest, wildest panic. Misadventures among the clouds he had had many times, and had looked a clean straight death in the face. He had never felt anything like the terror that for an instant possessed him. Then it passed and he said with conviction:

"Well, after all, there are certain things you can't be made to do against your will."

"Certainly. But you are not referring to marriage, are you?"

"Yes, I was."

"My poor, dear man! As if half the marriages in the world were not made against the wish of one party or the other."

His heart sank. "It's perfectly true," he said. "And yet one does rather hate to run away."

"Not so much as one hates afterward to think one might have."

He laughed and she went on: "The moment is critical. Laura Ussher and Christine have been closeted together for the better part of two hours. Something is going to happen immediately. At any moment Laura may appear and say with that wonderfully casual manner of hers, 'May I have a word with you, Max?' And then you'll be lost."

"Oh, not quite as bad as that, I hope," said Riatt.

"Lost," she repeated, and leaning over she laid one polished finger tip on the bell. "When the man comes, tell him to get you ready for that early train."

There was complete silence between them until the footman appeared and Riatt had given the necessary orders.

"I wonder," he said when they were again alone, "whether I shall be angry at you for this advice, or grateful. It's a dangerous thing, you know, to advise a man to run away."

"Dine with me in town on Wednesday, and you can tell me which it is."

"You don't seem to be much afraid of my anger."

"I think perhaps your gratitude might be the more dangerous of the two."

While he was struggling between a new-found prudence, and a natural desire to inquire further into her meaning, a door upstairs was heard to shut, and presently Laura Ussher came sauntering into the room.

"You're up early, Nancy," she said pleasantly.

"I thought I ought to recognize the return of the wanderers in some way—particularly, as I hear we are to lose one of them so soon."

Mrs. Ussher glanced quickly at her cousin. "Are you leaving us, Max?"

"I'm sorry to say I've just had word that I must, and I told the man to make arrangements for me to get that twelve-something-or-other train."

Mrs. Ussher did not change a muscle. "I'm sorry you have to go," she said. "We shall all miss you. By the way, you won't be able to get anything before the four-eighteen. That midday train is taken off in winter. Didn't the footman tell you? Stupid young man; but he's new and has not learnt the trains yet, I suppose. Do you want to send a telegram? They have to be telephoned here, but if you write it out I'll have it sent for you."

"How wonderful you are, Laura," murmured Mrs. Almar.

Mrs. Ussher looked vague. "In what way, dear?"

"In all ways, but I think it's as a friend that I admire you most."

Mrs. Ussher smiled. "Yes," she said, "I'm very devoted to my friends even when they don't behave quite fairly to me. But I love my relations, too," she added. "Max, since I'm to lose you so soon, I'd like to have a talk with you before lunch. Shall we go to my little study?"

Nancy's eyes danced. "No, Laura," she said, "he will not. He has just promised to teach me a new solitaire, and I won't yield him to any one."

Riatt, terrified at this proof that Nancy's prophecy was coming true, resolved to cling to her.

"Sit down and learn the game, too, Laura," he said. "It's a very good one."

"I want to speak to you about a business matter, Max."

"I never attend to business during church hours, Laura," he answered. "We'll talk about it after lunch, if you like."

Laura had learnt the art of yielding gracefully. "That will do just as well," she said, and sat down to watch the game.

Presently Wickham, seeing that Mrs. Almar seemed to be safely engaged, ventured back. And they were all thus innocently occupied when luncheon was announced.

Christine came down looking particularly lovely. It is a precaution which a good-looking woman rarely fails to take in a crisis. She was wearing a deep blue dress trimmed with fur, and only needed a solid gold halo behind her head to make her look like a Byzantine saint.

"Well, Miss Fenimer," said Wickham, as they sat down. "You look very blooming after your terrible experiences."

Christine had come prepared for battle. "Oh, they weren't so very terrible, Mr. Wickham, thank you," she said, and she leant her elbow on the table and played with those imitation pearls which she now hoped so soon to give to her maid. "Mr. Riatt is the most wonderful provider—expert as a cook as well as a furnace-man."

"It mayn't have been terrible for you," put in Ussher, who had a habit of conversational reversion, "but I bet it was no joke in the tool-house! How an intelligent woman like you, Christine, could dream of making a man spend the night in that hole, just for the sake of—"

"But I thought it was Mr. Riatt's own choice," said Nancy gently.

"You wouldn't think so if you could have felt the place," Ussher continued. "And what difference did it make? Who was there to talk? Every one knows that their being there was just an unavoidable accident—"

"Oh, if it had been an accident!" said Nancy, and it was as if a little venomous snake had suddenly wriggled itself into the conversation. Every one turned toward her, and her brother asked sternly:

"*If,* it had been an accident, Nancy? What the deuce do you mean by *if*?"

Nancy shook her small head. "I express myself badly," she said. "English rhetoric was left out of my education."

"You manage to convey your ideas, dear," said Laura.

"I was trying to say that if poor, dear Christine had not been so unfortunately the one to hit the horse in the head, and start him off—"

Wickham pricked up his ears. "Oh, I say, Miss Fenimer," he exclaimed, "did you really hit the horse?"

"Certainly, I did, Mr. Wickham."

"But what did you do that for?"

Christine did not trouble to answer this question. Hickson, who had been suffering far more than any one, rushed to the rescue.

"Miss Fenimer did not do it on purpose, Wickham. She happened to be standing—"

"Oh, is that what your sister meant?" said Christine, as if a sudden light dawned on her. "Tell me, Nancy darling, do you really think I hit the horse on purpose, so as to have an uninterrupted evening with Mr. Riatt? How you do flatter men! It's a great art. I'm afraid I shall never learn it."

For the first time, Riatt found himself looking at her with a certain amount of genuine admiration. This was very straight fighting. "They have the piratical virtues," he thought, "courage, and the ability to give and take hard blows."

Mrs. Almar was not to be outdone. "Well," she said, "I may as well be honest. I can imagine myself doing it, for the right man. And we should have had an amusing evening of it, which was more than we had here, I can tell you. We were very dreary. Mr. Wickham tried to relieve the monotony by a game of piquet, but I'm afraid he did not really enjoy it, for he has not asked me to play since." And she cast a quick stimulating glance at Wickham, whose usual inability to say nothing again betrayed him.

"Oh," he said, "I enjoyed our game immensely."

"Good," answered Nancy. "We'll have another this afternoon then."

"Indeed, yes," said Wickham, looking rather wan.

"After Mr. Riatt has gone," said Nancy distinctly. She knew that Laura had had no opportunity to convey this intelligence to Christine, and it amused her to see how she would support the blow. Christine's expression did not change, but her blue eyes grew suddenly a little darker. She turned slowly toward Riatt.

"And are you leaving us?" she asked.

"Sorry to say I am."

"What a bore," said Miss Fenimer politely. Hickson's simple heart bounded for joy. "She's refused him," he thought, "and that's why he's rushing off like this."

"Yes," said Ussher, "I should think he would want to go home and take some care of himself. It's a wonder if he doesn't develop pneumonia."

Christine smiled at Riatt across the table. "They make me feel as if I had been very cruel, Mr. Riatt," she said.

"Cruel, my dear," cried Nancy. "Oh, I'm sure you weren't *that*," and then intoxicated by her own success, she made her first tactical error. She turned to Riatt and said: "Don't forget that you are dining with me on Wednesday evening." She enjoyed this exhibition of power. She saw Laura and Christine glance at each other. But they were not dismayed; they saw at once that Max had not been playing his hand alone; he was going not entirely on his own initiative, and that was encouraging.

Riatt, who perfectly understood the public protectorate that was thus established over him, resented it; in fact by the time they rose from the table, he was thoroughly disgusted with all of them—weary, as he said to himself of their hideous little games. He hardened his heart even as Pharaoh did, and he felt not the least hesitation in according Laura the promised interview, for the reason that he felt no doubt of his own powers of resistance.

He permitted himself to be ostentatiously led away, upstairs to her little private sitting-room, with its books, and fireplace, and signed photographs, and he pretended not to see Nancy Almar's glance, which was almost a wink, and might have been occasioned by the fact that she herself was at the same moment gently guiding Wickham in the direction of a card-table.

Laura made her cousin very comfortable, in a long chair by the fire, with his cigarettes and his coffee beside him on a little table, and then she began murmuring:

"Isn't it a pity Nancy Almar is so poisonous at times! She isn't really bad hearted, but anything connected with Christine has always roused her jealousy—the old beauty and the new one, I suppose."

"I wonder," said Riatt, "what is the difference, if any, between a pirate and a bucaneer? Miss Fenimer and Mrs. Almar seem to me to have many qualities in common."

"Oh, Max, how can you say that? Christine is so much more gentle and womanly, so much—"

"My dear Laura, we haven't very much time, and I think you said you wanted to talk to me on a business matter."

Laura Ussher had the grace to hesitate, just an instant, before she answered: "Oh, yes, but it's your business I want to talk about. I want to speak to you about this terrible situation in which Christine finds herself. Do you realize that Nancy and Wickham between them will spread this story everywhere, with all the embellishments their fancy may dictate, particularly emphasizing the fact that it was Christine who made the horse run away. It will be in the papers within a week. You know, Max, just as well as I do, that it wasn't her fault. Is she to be so cruelly punished for it? Can you permit that?"

"It's not my fault either, Laura."

"You can so easily save the situation."

"How?"

"By asking her to marry you."

"That I will not do."

"Are you involved with some one else?"

"I might make you understand better if I said yes, but it would not be true. I'm not in love with any individual, but I know clearly the type of woman I could fall in love with, and it most emphatically is not Miss Fenimer's."

"Yet so many men have fallen in love with her."

"Oh, I see her beauty; I even feel her charm; but to marry her, no."

"Think of the prestige her beauty and position—"

"My dear Laura, what position? Social position as represented by the hectic triviality of the last few days? Thank you, no, again."

"Dear Max," said his cousin more seriously than she had hitherto spoken, "you know I would not want you to do anything that I thought would make you unhappy. But this wouldn't. I know Christine better than you do. I know that under all her worldliness and hardness there is a vein of devotion and sweetness—"

"Very likely there is. But it would not be brought out by a mercenary marriage with a man who cared nothing for her. If that is all you have to say, Laura, let's end an interview which hasn't been very pleasant for either of us."

"Oh, Max, how can you abandon that lovely creature to some tragic future?"

"You know quite well she is going to do nothing more tragic than to marry Hickson."

"And you are willing to sacrifice her to Hickson?"

"My dear Laura, I cannot prevent all the beautiful, dissatisfied women in the world from marrying dull, kind-hearted young men who adore them."

Mrs. Ussher stared at him in baffled, unhappy silence, and in the pause, the door quickly and silently opened and Christine herself entered. She looked calm, almost Olympian, as she laid her hand on Laura's arm.

"Let me have just a word alone with Mr. Riatt," she said; and as Laura precipitately left the room, Christine turned to Riatt with a reassuring smile. "Don't be alarmed," she said. "Your most dangerous antagonist has just gone. I've really come to rescue you." She sank into a chair. "How exhausting scenes are. Let me have a cigarette, will you?"

She smoked a moment in silence, while he stood erect and alert by the mantel-piece. At last, glancing up at him, she said:

"I suppose Laura was suggesting that you marry me?"

He nodded.

"Laura's a dear, but not always very wise. You see, she thinks we are both so wonderful, she can't believe we wouldn't make each other happy. And from her point of view, it is rather an obvious solution. You see, she does not know about that paragon in the Middle West."

"She existed only in my imagination."

"Oh, a dream-lady," said Christine, and her eyes brightened a little. "No wonder you thought her too good for Ned. Well, that brings me to what I came to tell you. I have decided to marry Edward Hickson."

There was a blank and rather flat pause, during which Riatt took his cigarette from his mouth and very carefully studied the ash, but could think of nothing to say. The thought in his mind was that Hickson was a dull dog.

"Have you told Hickson?" he asked after a moment.

She shook her head. "No, and I shan't till I get more accustomed to the idea myself. It isn't exactly an easy idea to get accustomed to. The prospect is not lively."

"I dare say you will contrive to make it as lively as possible."

She smiled drearily. "How very poorly you do think of me! I shan't make Ned a bad wife. He will be very happy, and Nancy and I will be like sisters. By the way, you're not in love with Nancy, are you?"

"Certainly not."

"Good. They all say it's a dog's life." She yawned. "Oh, isn't everything tiresome! If I had had any idea my filial deed in going to find my father's coat would have resulted in my having to marry Ned, I never would have gone."

Riatt struggled in silence. He wanted—any man would have wanted—to ask her whether there wasn't some other way out; but knowing that he himself was the only other way, he refrained and asked instead: "Is there anything I can do to help you?"

"There is," she responded promptly. "Rather a disagreeable thing, too. But it will be all over in an instant, and you can take your afternoon train and forget all about us. Will you do it?"

He hesitated, and she went on:

"Ah, cautious to the last! It's just a demonstration, a *beau geste*. It's this: You see, the situation, as I have discovered from a little talk with Ned, is more ugly than has yet appeared. They are holding one thing up their sleeve. Ned, it seems, noticed the track of your feet leaving the house, and it did not stop snowing until the morning. That was rather careless of you, wasn't it? Nancy can make a good deal of that one little fact."

"What people you are!"

"Rather horrid, aren't we? Did Laura keep telling you what a wonderful advantage it would be for you to be one of us? I wish I could have seen your face."

"Yes, she did say something of the advantages of belonging to a group like this. Do you know what any man who married you ought to do with you," he added with sudden vigor. "He ought to take you to the smallest, ugliest, deadest town he could find and keep you there five years."

"Thank you," she said. "You have achieved the impossible. You have made Ned seem quite exciting. Hitherto I have taken New York for granted, but now I shall add it to his positive advantages. But you haven't heard yet what it is I want you to do."

"What is it?"

"I want you to make me a well authenticated offer of marriage before you go for good."

"Miss Fenimer, I have the honor to ask you to marry me."

"I regret so much, Mr. Riatt, that a previous attachment prevents my accepting—but, my dear man, that isn't at all what I mean. Do you suppose Wickham and Nancy will believe me just because I walk out of this room and say you asked me to marry you? No, we must have some proof to offer."

"Something in writing?"

She hesitated.

"No," she said, "one really can't go about with a framed proposal like a college degree. I want a public demonstration."

"Something with a band or a phonograph?"

She was evidently thinking it out—or wished to appear to be. "Not quite that either. This would be more like it. Suppose I send for Nancy to come here now and consult with me as to whether I shall accept your offer or not. If I told her before you, she could hardly refuse to believe it. And you would be safe, for there isn't the least doubt what advice she will give me."

"You think she will advise you against me?"

Christine nodded. "She will try to save you from the awful fate she is reserving for her brother." She touched the bell. "Do you feel nervous?"

"A trifle," he answered, and indeed he did, for he knew better than Christine could, how strange this coming interview would appear to Mrs. Almar after the conversation before lunch. He consoled himself, however, by the thought that train-time was drawing near, "and then, please heaven," he said to himself, "I need never see any of them again."

"Isn't it strange," began Miss Fenimer, and then as a servant appeared in the doorway: "Oh, will you please ask Mrs. Almar to come here

ALICE DUER MILLER

for a few minutes and speak to me. Tell her it is very important. Isn't it strange," she went on, when the man had gone, "that I'm not a bit nervous, and yet I have so much more at stake than you have."

"You have a good deal clearer notion of your rôle than I."

"Your rôle is easy. You confirm everything I say, and contrive to look a little depressed at the end. Nothing could be simpler."

He hesitated. "Simpler than to look depressed when you refuse me?"

"No one really likes to be refused," she said. "Even I, hardened as I am, felt a certain distaste for the idea that Laura had been urging me on your reluctant acceptance. By the way, you did seem able to say no, after all your talk on our unfortunate drive about no man's being able to refuse a woman."

"Oh, a third party," he answered. "That's a very different thing. Had it been you yourself, with streaming eyes—" He looked at her sitting very cool and straight at a safe distance.

"I don't think I could cry to save my life," she observed. "Certainly not to save my reputation."

He did not answer. The situation had begun to seem like a game to him, or some absurd farce in which he was only reading some regular actor's part; and when presently the door opened to admit Mrs. Almar, he felt as if she had been waiting all the time in the wings.

Nancy stopped with a gesture of surprise, on finding that she was interrupting a tête-à-tête. Christine ignored her astonishment.

"Nancy dear," she said. "How nice of you to come, when I know how busy you were teaching Wickham piquet. Sit down. This is the reason I sent for you. As one of my best friends, I want your candid advice about this horrid situation."

"But Laura is one of your best friends, too," said Mrs. Almar.

"You'll see why I did not send for Laura. She is so ridiculously prejudiced in favor of Mr. Riatt. There's no question as to what her advice would be. In fact," said Christine with the frankest laugh, "she's advised it long ago—even before he asked me."

At these sinister words, Mrs. Almar gave a glance like the jab of a knife at Riatt.

"See here, Christine," she said, "every minute I spend here is a direct pecuniary loss to me. Let's get to the point."

"Of course. How selfish I am," answered Miss Fenimer. "The point is this. In view of the gossip and talk, and your own dear little suggestion, darling, that I had frightened the horse on purpose, Mr. Riatt has thought it necessary to ask me to marry him. I say he has thought it necessary, because in spite of all his flattering protestations, I can't help feeling that he's done it from a sense of duty. But whatever his sentiments may be, I've been quite open about mine. I'm not in love with him. In view of all this, Nancy, do you think it advisable that I accept his offer?"

Mrs. Almar had never been considered particularly good-tempered. Now she jumped to her feet with her eyes positively blazing. "Have I been called away from the care of my depleted bank account to take part in a farce like this?" she cried. "You ought to be ashamed of yourself, Christine. You know just as well as I do that that young man never even thought of asking you to marry him."

Christine was quite unruffled. "Oh, Nancy dear," she said, "how helpful you always are. I see what you mean. You think no one will believe that he ever did propose unless I accept him. I think you're perfectly right."

"They won't and I don't," said Nancy, and moved rapidly to the door.

"One moment, Mrs. Almar," said Riatt, firmly. "You happen to be mistaken. I did very definitely ask Miss Fenimer to marry me not ten minutes ago."

"And do you renew that request?" said Christine.

"I do."

Christine held out her hand with the gesture of a queen. "And I very gratefully accept your generous offer," she said.

"Well, heaven itself can't save a fool," said Mrs. Almar, and she went out of the room, and slammed the door after her.

As she went, Riatt actually flung the hand of his newly affianced wife from him. "May I ask," he said, "what you think you are doing?"

Christine had covered her face with her hands, and had sunk into a chair. For an instant Riatt really thought that the strain of the situation had been too much for her; but on closer inspection he found that she was shaking with laughter.

"I can't be sure which was funnier," she gasped, "your face or Nancy's."

Riatt did not seem to feel mirthful. "Do you take in," he asked her sternly, "that you have just broken your word."

"I've just plighted it, haven't I?"

"You promised to refuse me."

She sprang up. "I did not. I never said a word like it. If a stenographer had been here, the record would bear me out. You inferred it, I dare say.

Besides, what could I do? Even Nancy herself told us no one would believe us unless I accepted you—at least for a time."

"For what time?"

"Oh, don't let us cross bridges until we get to them. We are hardly engaged yet—Max! I must practise calling you Max, mustn't I?" In attempting to repress an irrepressible smile she developed an unknown dimple in her left cheek. The sight of it made his tone particularly relentless as he answered:

"If by the fifteenth of this month you have not broken this engagement, I'll announce its termination myself."

"And you," she went on, as if he had not spoken, "must get into the habit of calling me Christine."

"Listen to me," he said, and he took her by the shoulders with a gesture that no one could have mistaken for a caress. "I do not intend to marry you."

"I see you feel no doubt of my wishes in the matter."

"I wonder where I got the idea."

"Be reassured," she said, finding herself released. "My intentions are honorable. I would not marry any really nice man absolutely against his will. Although I did say to myself the very first time I saw you, coming downstairs in that well-cut coat of yours—or is it the shoulders?—I did say: 'I could be happy with that man, happier, that is, than with Ned.' You may think it isn't much of a compliment, but Ned has a very nice disposition, nicer than yours."

"And I should say it was the first requisite for your husband."

She became suddenly plaintive. "Of course I can see," she said, "why any one shouldn't want to be married, but I can't see why you object to being engaged to me for a few weeks."

"How can I be sure you will keep your word?"

"I'll give it to you in writing," she returned. "Write: This is to certify that I, Christine Fenimer, have enveigled the innocent and unsuspecting youth—"

"I won't," said Riatt.

"I will then," she answered, and sitting down she wrote:

"This is to certify that I, Christine Fenimer, have speciously, feloniously and dishonorably induced Mr. Max Riatt to make me an offer of marriage, which I knew at the time he had no wish to fulfil, and I hereby solemnly vow and swear to release him from same on or before the first day of March of this year of grace. (Signed) Christine Fenimer."

"There," she said, "put that in your pocketbook, and for goodness' sake don't let your pocket be picked between now and the first of March."

He took it and put it very carefully away, observing as he did so: "It's a long time to the first of March."

"It mayn't seem as long as you think."

"Are you by any chance supposing," he asked with a directness he had learnt from her own methods, "that by that time I may have fallen in love with you?"

She did not hesitate at all. "Well, I think it is a possibility."

"Oh, anything's possible, but I can tell you this: Even if I were in love with you, you are not the type of woman I should ever dream of marrying."

"What would you do?"

"If I saw the slightest chance of falling in love with you—which I don't—I should try all the harder to free myself."

"I don't see how you could try any harder than you have. You begin to make me suspicious."

"Miss Fenimer—"

"Christine, please."

"Christine, I am not the least bit in love with you."

"Quite sure that you're not whistling to keep your courage up?"

"Quite sure."

"Well," she said, "just to show my fair spirit, I'll tell you that I entirely believe you. Shall I add it to the contract: And I credit his repeated assertion that he is not and never will be in the least in love with me? No, I think I'll omit the 'and never will be' clause."

"And may I ask one other question," he continued, ignoring her last suggestion. "What did you mean when you told me that you had decided to marry Hickson?"

"So I have. Don't you see? He and I are really engaged, but he doesn't know it. You and I are not really engaged, and you *do* know it."

"I wish I did," he returned gloomily.

"Oh, yes," she said, "you know it and I know it, but the dog—that's Nancy—she doesn't know it."

He seemed unimpressed by the humor of the situation. He walked away and put his hand on the knob.

"One thing more," he said. "I would like to be sure that you understand this. The weapons are all in my hands. The only strength of your position lies in my good nature and willingness to keep up appearances. Neither one is a rock of defense. I'm not, as you said yourself, good-tempered, and I care very little for appearances. The risk you run, if you don't play absolutely fair, is of being publicly jilted."

"And I should hate that," she answered candidly.

"I'm sure you would," he answered. "And I don't particularly enjoy threatening you with such a possibility."

"Really," said she. "Now I rather like you when you talk like that."

"Fortunate that you do," he returned, "for you will probably hear a good deal of it."

She nodded with perfect acquiescence. "And now," she said, "if you have no more hateful things to say, let's go and tell our friends of the great happiness that has come into our lives."

IV

As they went down the stairs—those same stairs on which only two evenings before they had first met—toward the drawing-room where their great announcement was to be made, Riatt stopped Christine in her triumphal progress.

"You're not going to have the supreme cruelty," he said, "to let poor Hickson think that our engagement is a genuine one?"

Christine paused. "I wonder," she answered thoughtfully, "which in the end would deceive him most—to make him think it was real or fake?"

"You blood-curdling woman," said Riatt. "I am not engaged to you."

"Oh, yes, you are—until March first."

"I am pretending to be until March first."

She leant against the banisters, and regarded him critically. "Isn't it strange," she remarked, "that you dislike so much the idea of my trying to make you care for me? Some men would be crazy about the process."

"Oh, if I enjoyed the process, I should regard myself as lost."

She shook her head. "I'm not sure that this terror isn't a more significant confession of weakness. Who is it is most afraid of high places? Those who feel a desire to jump off."

"I'm not afraid," he returned crossly. "I just don't like it. I don't want to be made love to. That's one of the mistakes women are always making. They think all men want to be made love to by any woman. We don't."

Christine sighed gently. "You're getting disagreeable again," she said with the softest reproach in her tone. "Let's go on."

"You haven't answered my question," he said. "Are you going to tell Hickson the truth?"

"How can I? If I told him, Nancy would know at once, and the whole aim of this plot is to deceive Nancy. However," she added brightly, "I shall do what I can to alleviate his sufferings. I shall tell him that I am not in the least in love with you, that you have never so much as kissed me, and that my present intention is that you never shall."

"And you may add that my intention is the same," replied Riatt with some sternness.

Christine smiled. "There's no use in telling him that," she answered, "for he wouldn't believe it."

"Upon my word," said he, "I think you're the vainest woman I ever met."

"Candid, merely," she returned, as she opened the door of the drawing-room. The scene that greeted them was eminently suited to their purpose. Laura and Ussher were standing at the table watching the last bitter moments of the game between Nancy and the unfortunate Wickham. Hickson was not there.

"Oh, Laura," said Christine, "could I have just a word with you?"

Mrs. Ussher looked up startled. She had been deeply depressed by her unsuccessful conversation with her cousin. He had seemed to her absolutely immovable, but there was no mistaking the significant bride-like modulations of Christine's voice.

"With me?" she said, and in her eagerness she was already at the door, before Christine stopped her.

"Really," she said, "I don't know why only with you. I know you are all enough my friends to be interested—even Mr. Wickham. Max and I wanted to tell you that we are engaged. Only, of course, it's a secret."

Riatt had resolved that he would not look at Mrs. Almar, and he didn't. She was adding up the score, and her arithmetic did not fail her. "And that makes 387, Mr. Wickham," she said, and then she looked up with her bright, piercing eyes, in time to see Laura fling herself enthusiastically into Riatt's arms. She got up with a shrewd smile. "Let me congratulate you, too, Mr. Riatt," she said. "I always like to see people get what they deserve."

"Oh, Nancy, I'm sure you think I'm getting far more than I deserve," said Christine.

"You haven't actually got it yet, darling," returned Mrs. Almar.

"That sounds almost like a threat, my dear."

"More in the line of a prophecy."

At this moment the footman created a diversion by announcing that the sleigh was waiting to take Mr. Riatt to the train, and Riatt explained that he had decided not to take the train that day. Then Christine, on inquiring, found that Hickson was writing letters in the library, and went away to talk to him. She had no fear of leaving Max; she knew he was in safe hands; Laura would not allow Nancy an instant alone with him. Nor, as a matter of fact, was Riatt himself eager to subject himself to the cross-examination of that keen and contemptuous intelligence. Indeed Nancy soon drifted out of the room, and Riatt found himself committed to a long tête-à-tête with Laura on the subject of Christine's perfections, and his supposed deceitfulness in pretending indifference. "Oh, you protested too much, my dear Max," Laura insisted with the most irritating exuberance. "I knew when you began to say that she was the last woman in the world you would fall in love with, that your hour had come. No man ever lived who could resist Christine when she chooses to make herself agreeable."

Riatt felt he was looking rather grim for an accepted lover, as he answered that it was a great comfort to feel one had succumbed only to the irresistible. Before very long Christine came back, and taking in what had been going on, managed to get rid of her friend. Laura made it plain that she was only too glad to accord the lovers a few blissful moments alone.

"I can't describe to you," he said crossly, "how intensely disagreeable I find the situation."

Christine laughed. "And did you look like that while Laura was detailing my perfections? A judge about to pronounce the death sentence is gay in comparison. Cheer up. I haven't had a pleasant fifteen minutes myself. I never thought myself kind-hearted, but I assure you I really longed to tell Ned the truth. He is the nicest person."

"I believe he will make you an excellent husband."

"Oh, dear, I'm afraid he will." She sighed. "Safety first will be a dull motto to go through life with. Do you want to know what I told him? No? Well, I'm going to tell you anyhow. I said that you had made me this magnificent offer, prompted, I felt sure, by the purest chivalry; and that I felt I owed it to my family, my friends and my reputation to accept it, but that you had left my heart untouched, and that if he and you were both penniless, I should prefer him to you. That wasn't all perfectly true."

Suddenly Riatt found himself smiling. "My innocent child," he said, "let me make one thing clear to you. Any effort on your part to create an impression that you have fallen in love with me will not be crowned with success."

Christine was quite unabashed by his directness.

"I'm not a bit in love with you," she said—"not any more than you are with me, only I realize that there is a possibility for either of us, and of the two," she added maliciously, "I really think I'm the more hard-hearted."

"Perhaps you will think I am running away from danger," he answered, "when I tell you that as soon as I have seen your father, got your ring, and fulfilled the immediate necessities of the occasion, I shall go home."

ALICE DUER MILLER

"Oh, you can't do that!" cried Christine, in genuine alarm.

"You surely don't expect me to neglect my legitimate business on account of this ridiculous farce."

For the first time a certain amount of real hostility crept in their relation. They looked at each other steadily. Then Christine said politely: "Well, we'll see how things go." He knew, however, that she was as determined that he should stay as he was to leave, and the knowledge made him all the firmer.

The evening was a stupid one, devoted largely to toasts, jokes, congratulations and a few stabs from Nancy. Through it all poor Hickson's gloom was obvious.

The next day the party broke up. Wickham and Hickson taking an early express; the others, even Nancy who abandoned her motor on account of the snow, going in by a noonday train. Already, it seemed to Riatt that the bonds of matrimony were closing about him as he found himself delegated to look up Christine's trunks, maid and dressing-case.

Soon after the arrival of the train he had an appointment, made by telephone, with Mr. Fenimer. The interview was to take place at Mr. Fenimer's club, a most discreet and elegant organization of fashionable virility. Riatt was not kept waiting. Fenimer came promptly to meet him.

He was a man of fifty, well made, and supremely well dressed. He was tanned as befits a sportsman; on his face the absence of furrows created by the absence of thought was made up for by the fine wrinkles induced by poignant and continued anxiety about his material comforts. In his figure the vigor of the athlete contended with the comfortable stoutness of the epicure. He had left a discussion in which all his highest faculties had been roused, a discussion on the replenishing of the club's cellar, and had come to speak to his future son-in-law, with satisfaction but without vital interest. His manner was a perfect blending of reserve and cordiality.

"You will hardly expect a definite answer from me today, Mr. Riatt," he said. "You understand, I am sure, that knowing so little of you— an only child, my daughter"—He waved his hand, not manicured but most beautifully cared for. Riatt noticed that in spite of these chilling sentences, Fenimer was soon composing a paragraph for the press, and advocating the setting of the date for the wedding early in April, as he himself was booked for a fishing-trip later. He did this under the assumption that he was yielding to Riatt's irresistible eagerness. "You have an excellent advocate in Christine. My daughter has always ruled me. And now in my old age I am to lose her. I had a long letter from her by the early mail, speaking of you in the highest terms." He smiled. Riatt rose, and allowed him to return to the question of the club's wines.

Something about this interview was more shocking to him than the cynicism of Nancy and Christine; Fenimer's suave eagerness to hand his daughter over to a total stranger, did not amuse him as the women's light talk had done. He felt sorry for Christine and a little disgusted. He wondered what that letter had really said. Was Fenimer a conspirator, too, or only a willing dupe?

From the club he went to the jeweler's and selected the most conspicuous diamond he could find. Her friends should not miss the fact that she was engaged if a solitaire could prove it to them. He ordered it sent to her, much to the surprise of the clerk, who pointed out that it was usual to present such things in person.

After this he went to his hotel and found a pile of letters had accumulated in his absence.

The first he opened was in a round childish hand with uncertain margins, and a final "e" on the word Hotel.

"Dear Cousin Max," it said, "I do not know you, but Mamma
says that you are going to marry Christine. I think you are
very lucky, and am glad you are bringing her into our family.
Victor and I love her. She comes to the nursery sometimes,
but never stays long.

Your loving cousin,
MURIEL USSHER

Riatt laughed as he laid it down. "I bet she doesn't stay long," he said. "How she does skim the cream!" And then with an exclamation of surprise he tore open another envelope which had been left by hand. It said:

Dear Max:
"I hope you will be pleasantly surprised to find that
Mother and I are staying in this hotel. I find New York more
wonderful but more unfriendly than I had been told, and I
want terribly to see a familiar face. Won't you look us up as
soon as you can?

Yours as ever,
DOROTHY

ALICE DUER MILLER

He went to the telephone, found that she was in and immediately arranged that she should go out to lunch with him.

All the morning and some of the night, he had been engaged in the composition of a letter to Dorothy Lane. Theirs was an old and sentimental friendship, which adverse circumstances might have ended, or favoring circumstances have changed into love. As things were, it seemed to be tending toward their marriage without any whirlwind rapidity.

There was no doubt he was very glad to see her, as he hurried her into a taxicab, and told the man to drive to the restaurant of the hour. She was very neatly and nicely dressed in a tailor-made costume for which she had just paid twice as much as a native New York woman would have paid. In fact she was an essentially neat and nice little person. They talked both at once like two children about all the people at home, until they were actually seated at table, and lunch was ordered. Then Riatt made up his mind he must take the plunge.

"Dolly," he said, "do I look as if something tremendous had just happened?"

"Don't tell me you've invented a submarine, or something?"

"No, this is something of a more personal nature."

"Oh, Max, you've fallen in love?"

A waiter rushing up with rolls and butter suggested that Madame probably preferred fresh butter to salted, before Riatt answered: "No, that is just what I haven't done—and that's the secret, Dolly. I'm not a bit in love, but I am engaged to be married."

"Max! But why if—"

"I'll tell you on the second of March. It's a good story. You'll enjoy it, but for the present, my dear, you must just accept the fact that I am engaged, that I am neither wildly elated nor unduly depressed."

Miss Lane had grown extremely serious. "Who is she?" she asked.

"Her name is Christine Fenimer."

"I've seen her name in the papers."

"Who has not?" he returned bitterly.

"What is she like?"

Riatt felt some temptation to answer truthfully and say: "She is designing, mercenary, hard-hearted and as beautiful as a goddess." But he did not, and, as he paused he saw the head waiter spring forward from the doorway, smiling and holding up a pencil to attract the attention of some underling, and then he saw that Christine,

Hickson and Mr. and Mrs. Linburne were being ushered in. Christine approached, tall, beautiful, conspicuous, and as divinely unconscious of it as Adam and Eve of their nakedness; she moved between the tables, bowing here and there to people she knew, not purposely ignoring all others, but seeming to find them invisible as thin air. Riatt watched as if she were some great spectacle, and was recalled only by hearing Dorothy's voice saying:

"What a lovely creature!"

"That is Miss Fenimer."

A sudden and deep flush spread over Miss Lane's face.

"And you have been telling me of your indifference to her?" she asked bitterly. "How could any man be indifferent!"

"Good Heavens," cried Riatt fiercely. "All you women are alike! Beauty isn't the only thing in the world for a man to love. There are such things as truth and honor—"

"Yes, and old friendship, too," said Miss Lane, "but they don't always amount to much."

"That is an unnecessary, unkind thing to say," he answered. "My friendship for you means a good deal more to me than my engagement to her."

"Max, I don't need to be consoled or soothed about your engagement," said Miss Lane with a good deal of spirit. "As far as I am concerned you are quite free not only to become engaged, but to have any feeling you like for the lady you have chosen. I'm sure I congratulate you very heartily."

"You mean you don't believe a word of what I have been trying to tell you."

"Oh, yes, I do. I believe you are engaged."

Perhaps it was as well that at this instant, Christine's eyes fell upon her; she stared, then laughed, and pointed him out to Hickson, who glanced at him coldly; he was evidently thinking that he would not have taken another girl out to lunch the very day his engagement was announced.

"I suppose I had better go and speak to them," Max said.

"I should think so," replied Dorothy tonelessly. "Who are the others?"

Riatt, not sorry for a moment's respite, entered into a detailed account of Lee Linburne. He was the third generation of a great fortune, augmenting rather than decreasing with years. He was but little over thirty and had taken the whole field of amusement and sports as his

ALICE DUER MILLER

own. He played polo, had a racing stable and a racing yacht, had gone in recently for flying (hence Riatt's connection with him), occasionally financed a theatrical show, and now and then attended a directors' meeting of some of his grandfather's companies. The result was that his name was as widely known through the country as Abraham Lincoln's. Dorothy knew as soon as she heard his name, that he had married a girl from Pittsburg, and had gone through her native city in a private car on his honeymoon three years before, and had stopped, she rather thought, and had lunch with the Governor of the State.

On Hickson, Max touched more briefly.

When at last he did cross the room, Christine received him with the utmost cordiality.

"What luck to run across you, though of course this is the only place in New York where one can get food that doesn't actually poison one. Last week—do you remember, Lee? We dined somewhere or other with the Petermans and nothing from the beginning of dinner to the end was fit to eat. But, bless them, they did not know. Have you met Mrs. Linburne? Oh, she knows all about *us*. In fact every one does, for I can't resist wearing this." She moved her left hand on which his diamond shone like a swollen star. "How did you find my father?"

"Most amiable," answered Riatt rather poisonously, and regretted the poison when he saw the Linburnes exchange an amused glance. Of course every one knew that Mr. Fenimer would present no obstacles.

"Who are you lunching with, Max? Is that your little secretary?"

The tone, very civil and friendly, made Max furious, as if any one that Christine did not know was hardly worth inquiring about.

"No, it's Miss Lane—an old friend of mine. I think I must have spoken to you about her."

"Oh, the perfect provider? Is that really she?" Christine craned her neck openly to stare at her. "Why, she's rather nice looking—for a good housekeeper, that is. You're dining with me tonight, aren't you?"

"No," answered Riatt, with a sudden inspiration of ill-humor. "I'm dining with Miss Lane."

"Bring her, too! Won't she come?"

"I really can't say."

"You can ask her."

"To your house?"

Christine always knew when she was really beaten. She got up with a sigh. "Take me over," she said to him, "and I'll ask her myself." And she added to the Linburnes: "Out-of-town people are always so fussy about little things."

Riatt did not know if this slightly contemptuous observation were meant to apply to him or to Miss Lane; he hoped in his heart that Dorothy would refuse the invitation. But he under-estimated Christine's powers. No one could have been more persuasive, more meltingly sweet, and compellingly cordial than she was, and it was soon arranged that he was to bring Dorothy to dine that evening.

When it was over, and he was back again in his own seat, he could see, by glancing at Christine that she was engaged in a long humorous account of the incident, for her own table; and he could tell, even from that distance, when he was supposed to be speaking, when Dorothy, and when Christine was repeating her own words. Meanwhile Dorothy was saying:

"How charming and simple she is, Max. You always hear of these people as being so artificial and elaborate."

"Oh, they're direct enough," returned Riatt bitterly.

The bitterness was so apparent that Dorothy could not ignore it. She looked up at him for an instant and then she said seriously: "I believe I know what the trouble with you is, Max. You can't believe that she loves you for yourself. You're haunted by the dread that what you have has something to do with it. Isn't that it?"

Max now made use of the well-known counter question as an escape from a tight place.

"And what is your judgment on that point, Dolly?"

"She loves you," said Miss Lane, with conviction, and a moment afterward she sighed.

"Without disputing your opinion," returned Riatt, "I should very much like to know on what you base it."

"Oh, on a hundred things—on her look, her manner, her being so nice to me—on woman's intuition in fact."

Riatt thought to himself that he had never had much confidence in the intuition theory and now he had none.

They did not part at the termination of lunch. It was almost a duty, Riatt considered, to show a stranger a few of the sights. Miss Lane, who was extremely well-informed on all questions of art, suggested the Metropolitan Museum; and after that they took a taxicab and drove along the river and watched the winter sunset above the palisades; and then they went and had tea at the Plaza, and by the time they returned to Mrs. Lane

ALICE DUER MILLER

it was almost the hour for dressing for dinner; and then Max sat gossiping with Mrs. Lane, for whom he had always had the deepest affection, until he knew he was going to be late.

They were late—a difficult thing to be in the Fenimer household. The party, a small one, was waiting when Miss Lane and Mr. Riatt were ushered in. Nancy was there, and Hickson, and Mr. Linburne without his wife this time; and Mr. Fenimer himself, doing honor to his future son-in-law by taking a meal at home.

Christine in a wonderful pink chiffon and lace tea-gown came forward to greet Dorothy, rather than Max, to whom she gave merely an understanding smile, while she held the girl's hand an instant.

"Max says this is your first visit to New York," she said, after she had introduced her father and Nancy. "It is good of you to give us an evening, when there are so many more amusing things to do, but Max says we are as interesting as Bushmen or Hottentots. I hope you'll find us so."

The hope seemed unlikely to be fulfilled, for while the presence of Mr. Fenimer, who was rather a stickler for etiquette, prevented the perfect freedom that had reigned at the Usshers', the talk turned on people whom Dorothy did not know, and it was so quick and allusive that no outsider could have followed it. Hickson, soon appreciating something in Miss Lane's situation not utterly unlike his own, was touched by her obvious isolation, and tried to make up for the neglect of the others. Riatt, sitting between Nancy and Christine, had little time left to him for observation of any one else.

When dinner was over Christine instantly drew him away to her own little sitting-room, on pretense of showing him some letter of congratulation that she had received. But once there, she shut the door, and standing before it, she said, with an air of the deepest feeling:

"You're in love with this girl."

Riatt, who had sunk comfortably down on a sofa by the fire, looked up in surprise.

"And if I am?" he answered.

"You need not humiliate me by making it so evident," she retorted, and almost stamped her foot. "Lunching with her in public, and taking her to tea, as I was told, getting here so late for dinner—I wish you could have heard the way Nancy and Lee Linburne were goading me before dinner about it."

"My dear Christine," said Max, and he was amused to hear a tone of real conjugal remonstrance in his voice, "you have lunched and dined in one day with Hickson, and yet I don't feel I have any grounds of complaint."

"Every one knows how little I care for Ned," she answered, "but people say you do care for this little Western mouse. I hate her. She's good and nice, and the kind of a girl men think it wise to marry, and just as different from me as she can be. I do hate her—and I hate myself too." And she covered her face with her hands.

"Come here, Christine," said Riatt, without moving, and was rather surprised when she obeyed. He made her sit down beside him, and taking her hands from her face, was astonished to find that she was really crying.

"Why, my dear child," he said, in the most paternal manner he could manage. "What is this all about?" And it was quite in the same note that Christine wept a moment on his shoulder. Then she raised her head, with a return of her old brisk manner.

"I'm jealous," she said. "Oh, don't suppose one can't be jealous of people one doesn't care for. I could be jealous of any one when Nancy begins teasing me and making fun of me. And I'm jealous too, because I'm sure she's a nice girl and I've made such a mess of my life, and I deserve it all; but when you came in together, as if you had just been happily married, and I looked at Ned and thought how wretched I'm always going to be with him, and what silly things I shall undoubtedly do before I die—"

"I hate to hear you talk like that."

"Why should you care? *She'll* never do silly things—that's clear. Is that why you love her?"

"As a matter of fact I am not in love with Miss Lane."

"My dear Max, there's really no reason why you should deceive me about it."

"That's just what she said about you."

"You mean"—Christine sprang to her feet and gazed at him like an outraged empress—"You mean that you told her that you didn't love me?"

"I most assuredly did."

"Max, how could you be so low, so despicable, so false?"

Riatt laughed. "Well, it certainly was not false, Christine," he said. "It happens to be true, you know; and I felt I owed a measure of truth to a very old and very real friendship. I told her nothing more than that—I was engaged and not madly in love."

ALICE DUER MILLER

Christine threw up her hands. "The game is up," she said. "She'll tell everybody, of course."

"She'll tell absolutely no one."

"Because she's perfect, I suppose?"

"Because she didn't for one moment believe me."

"Didn't believe we were engaged?"

"Didn't believe that any one could be engaged to so beautiful and charming a person as you are and not be in love with her."

Christine's manner softened slightly. "She thinks me charming?"

"She thinks you irresistible, almost as irresistible as Laura thinks you; and she is trying to find out why I am so eager to deceive her in the matter."

Christine clapped her hands, and executed a few steps. "She's jealous, too," she cried. "The perfect woman is jealous. I never thought of her suffering, too."

"She is not jealous, but I suppose it may hurt her feelings a little that I shouldn't—"

"Oh, nonsense, Max, she loves you. Do you think I could be deceived on such a subject? She watches you all the time. She loves you. And I think it would be very impertinent of her not to. I should think very poorly of her if she didn't. Imagine what she must be undergoing at this moment, by our prolonged absence."

"Perhaps, we'd better be going back," said Riatt calmly.

Christine barred the door, spreading out both her arms.

"She thinks you're making love to me, Max."

"And yet, Christine, I'm not."

"But she doesn't know that; she doesn't know what an immovable iceberg you are."

"No, indeed she doesn't."

Christine's manner again changed utterly. All the playfulness disappeared. "You mean," she said, "that you're not cold and immovable with her?"

"What's the use of my telling you anything, if you don't believe me?" The idea of teasing Christine had never occurred to him before, but he thought highly of it. She came toward him at once.

"Oh, Max, my dear," she said, "don't be horrid, when I'm having such a wretched time anyhow. Don't you think you might *pretend* to care for me just a little?"

Riatt rose. "Yes, I do," he said, "and so I shall, in public."

Christine was all the gentle, wistful child immediately.

"Never when we're alone?" she asked.

Max lit a cigarette briskly. "I don't suppose we shall very often be alone," he returned. "After all, why should we?"

She looked at him like a wounded bird: "No reason if you don't want to."

At this moment the door opened and her father came in.

"Come, come, my dear, this is no way to treat your guests," he said. "I must really insist that you go back to the drawing-room. Upon my word, Riatt, you ought not to keep her like this."

"It was a great temptation to have her a few minutes to myself, Mr. Fenimer," said Max, and Christine grinned gratefully at him behind her father's back.

"Very likely, very likely," said Mr. Fenimer crossly, "but I want to go to the club, and how can I, unless she goes back? You can't think only of yourself, my dear fellow."

Riatt admitted that this was true and he and Christine went back to the drawing-room.

Very soon afterwards, he gave Dorothy a keen prolonged look, which she did not misunderstand. She got up at once and said good night. In the taxicab, he questioned her at once as to her impressions.

"I didn't like Mr. Linburne or Mrs. Almar at all, Max. She kept asking me the greatest number of questions about you and the story of your life. What interest has she in you, I wonder?"

"None," answered Riatt, but added rather quickly, "And what did you think of Linburne?"

"I couldn't bear him, though I own he's nice looking. But he told Mrs. Almar a story—I could not help hearing—I never heard such a story in my life."

"I gather it did not shock Mrs. Almar."

"She knew it already. 'Lee,' she said, 'that story is so old that even my husband knows it,' and every one laughed."

"I'm afraid you did not enjoy yourself."

"I like Mr. Hickson very much. And I thought Miss Fenimer more beautiful than before. He was telling me what a wonderful nature she has. He said he had never seen her out of temper."

"Yes, Hickson's crazy about her," said Riatt casually.

"Dear Max, why do you try to deceive yourself about your own feeling for her?"

"Deceive myself," he said angrily. "If you knew the truth, my dear Dolly!" His heart stood still. Deceive himself! What an insulting phrase. He repressed a strong impulse to propose on the instant to Dolly. That would show her how indifferent he was to Christine. It would assure him, too.

Instead he formed a plan to go home with her and her mother, when they went.

"When are you going back, Dolly?"

"The day after tomorrow."

"Any objections to my going, too?"

"Objections! Max, dear!"

He engaged his ticket at once at the hotel office. Having done so, he felt tranquil and relieved, and perhaps the least little bit dull. The clerk assured him he was fortunate to be able to get a berth at such short notice. "Very fortunate," he agreed and was annoyed at a certain cold ring in his voice.

The next day, true to his promise to show Christine all attentions that the public could expect, he sent her a box of flowers, and at four he stopped for her and they went and took a long walk together, hoping to meet as many people whom they knew as possible.

"We won't walk in the Park," said Christine. "No one sees you there, though of course if they do, it makes an impression. But, no; we'll stick to Fifth Avenue, and study all the windows that have clothes or furniture in them, as if our minds were entirely taken up with trousseaux and house-furnishing."

She was true to her word, and not squeamish. Riatt found it rather amusing to wander at her side, dressing her in imagination in every garment that the windows so frankly displayed, and answering with real interest her constant inquiry: "Do you think that would become me? Would you like me in that? Do you prefer silk to batiste?"

They were standing in front of a stocking shop in which on a row of composition legs which might have made a chorus envious, "new ideas in hosiery" were romantically displayed, when Riatt decided to tell her of his approaching departure. He chose the street, because he was well aware that she would not approve of his plan, and he wished to avoid a repetition of last evening's scene.

"I shall have to go away the day after tomorrow," he said, and glanced quickly down on her to see how she would take it.

She was studying the stockings, and she drew away with her head at a critical angle.

"It's a queer thing," she said, "that certain stripes do make the ankle look large. Theoretically they ought to make it look slim, but you take my word for it, Max, they don't."

"Nothing could make your ankles look anything but slim, Christine," he replied politely.

"No, my ankles are rather good, aren't they?" she replied, and then as if she had now disposed of the more serious topic, she added: "And so you are going home? Well, you mayn't believe it, but I shall really miss you a great deal. Oh, look at these jade flowers! They're really good."

Riatt looked at the pale lilac and pink blossoms starting from their icy green leaves, but he hardly saw them. He was disgusted at the discovery of an unexpected perversity in his nature. He found himself hardly pleased at the absence of protest with which his announcement was greeted. All her attention was absorbed by the jade.

"Wouldn't it look well on our drawing-room mantel-piece?" she said.

"I'll give it to you as a wedding present," he answered. "That is, if you think Hickson would like it."

"I don't think he'll like anything you ever give me. He did not even like my ring. He thinks the stone too large. By the way, I never properly thanked you for the ring. It has been most splendidly persuasive. Even Nancy grew pale when she saw the proof of your sincerity."

"Will it be sufficient even in the face of my continued absence?" he asked, for it occurred to him that perhaps she had not understood that he meant to remain in the West indefinitely.

"Oh, I think so," she answered, pleasantly. "You might write to me now and then, and I'll show just a suitable paragraph here and there to an intimate friend."

A new idea suddenly occurred to him. Had she any motive for desiring his absence? Had some unexpected possibility cropped up? Did she want to get rid of him? Not, he added, that he minded if she did, but it would be rather interesting to know.

"I'm going a little earlier than I expected," he went on, "because the Lanes are going, and I hate to make that long journey alone."

She nodded understandingly. "It will be much nicer for you to have them."

He looked at her coldly. It seemed to him he had never known a more callous nature. And to think that the evening before she had actually shed tears, simply because he took another girl to lunch! It caught his attention, he said to himself, just as a study in human nature.

He did not see her the next day until evening. They were both to dine at Nancy's—(thus had the proposed dinner with Mrs. Almar deteriorated) and go afterward to the opera. Nancy of course would not have dreamed of crowding three women into her box, so the party consisted of herself and Christine, Riatt, Roland Almar—a pale, eager, little man, trying to placate the world with smiles, and once again Linburne, whose handsome dark head, and curved mouth, half cynical, half sensuous, began to weary Riatt inexpressibly.

After dinner he found that he and Mrs. Almar were to go in her tiny coupé, and the four others in Linburne's large car.

"And so," she observed as soon as they started, "the mouse preferred the trap after all?" And he could feel that she was laughing at him in the shadow.

"But feels none the less grateful for the kind intention to rescue him."

"Oh, I don't care much for the gratitude of a man in love with another woman."

"You judge me to be very much in love?"

This general conviction on the part of the ladies of his acquaintance was growing monotonous. Nancy continued:

"But come back in two years, and we'll talk of gratitude then. In the meantime let us stick to the impersonal. What do you think of Linburne?"

"I've had many opportunities of judging. I've been nowhere for two days without meeting him."

Mrs. Almar laughed with meaning.

"I wonder why that should be," she said.

"What do you mean?" Riatt asked, but at that moment they drew up before the Thirty-ninth Street entrance, and the doorman, opening the motor's door, shouted "Ten—Forty-five"—a cheerful lie he has been telling four times a week for many years.

In the opera box, Riatt at once seated himself behind Christine. There is no place like the opera for public devotion. Christine was resplendent in black and gold with a huge black and gold fan that made the fans of the temple dancers—the opera was "Aïda"—look commonplace and ineffective.

Behind it she now murmured to Max:

"And what poisonous thing did dear Nancy tell you coming down?"

"Nothing—except what everyone has been telling me for the last few days—that I seemed very much in love."

"And that annoyed you, I suppose."

"On the contrary. I was delighted to find I was such a good actor."

"People who pretend to be asleep sometimes end by actually doing it. Pretending is rather dangerous sometimes."

"Yes, but you see I shan't have to pretend after tomorrow."

"Are you all packed and ready?"

"Mentally I am."

In the *entr'acte* which followed quickly after their entrance, Christine dismissed him very politely. "There," she said, "you don't have to stay on duty all the time. You can go and stretch your legs, if you want."

He rose at once, and as he did so, Linburne slipped into his place.

Riatt had caught sight of Laura Ussher across the house, and knew his duty demanded that he should go and say a word to his exuberant cousin who, he supposed, regarded herself as the artificer of his happiness.

"Oh, my dear Max," she began, hastily bundling out an old friend who had been reminiscing about the days of the de Rezskes, and waving Riatt into place, "every one is so delighted at the engagement, and thinks you both so fortunate. How happy she is, Max! She looks like a different person."

"I thought she looked rather tired this evening," answered Riatt, who always found himself perverse in face of Laura's enthusiasm.

Mrs. Ussher raised her opera glass and studied Christine's profile, bent slightly toward Linburne, who was talking with the immobility of feature which many people use when saying things in public which they don't wish overheard. "Oh, well, she doesn't look as brilliant as she did when *you* were with her. But isn't that natural? I wonder why Nancy asked Lee Linburne and where is that silly little wife of his. Oh, don't go, Max. It's only the St. Anna attaché; we met him on the coast last summer."

But Riatt insisted on making way for the South American diplomat, who was standing courteously in the back of the box.

He wandered out into the corridors, not enough interested in any of his recent acquaintances to go and speak to them. Two men coming up behind him were talking; he could not help hearing their dialogue:

"Who's this fellow she's engaged to?"

"No one knows—a Western chap with a lot of money."

"Suppose she cares anything about him?"

"Oh, no, she's telling every one she doesn't. They say he's mad about her."

"Ought to be, by Jove. I always thought the only man she ever cared for—"

Riatt found himself straining his ears vainly to catch the name, but it was drowned in other conversations that rose about him. He understood now why Christine had been angry at his telling Dorothy that he was not in love, for he found himself annoyed at the idea of her having told everybody that she wasn't. But, it's a different thing, he thought, to tell one intimate friend in confidence, or to give the news to every Tom, Dick and Harry. Then the juster side of his nature reasserted itself, and he saw that she was only laying the trail for the breaking of her engagement. Yet this evidence of her good faith did not entirely allay the irritation of his spirit.

When he went back to the box, Linburne was gone, and the man who had replaced him, yielded to Riatt with the most submissive promptness. But this time no easy interchange occurred between them.

About half past ten, Christine leaned over to her hostess, and said: "Would you care at all if I deserted you, dear? I'm tired."

"Mind when I have my Roland to keep me company?" said Nancy. "One seems to take one's husband to the opera this year."

At this point Linburne, who had been standing in the back of the box, came forward and said: "Won't you take my car, Miss Fenimer? I'll go down and find it for you."

A look that passed between them, a twinkle in Nancy's eyes, suddenly convinced Riatt that the scheme was for Linburne to take Christine home. He did not stop to ask why this idea was repugnant to him, but he said firmly:

"I have a car of my own downstairs, and I'll take Miss Fenimer home." It was of course a lie, as the simple taxicab was his only means of vehicular locomotion, but a taxi, thank heaven, can always be obtained quickly at the Metropolitan. Christine consented. Linburne stepped back.

They drove the few blocks in silence. He went up the steps of her house, and when the door was opened he said: "May I come in for a few minutes? I shan't have time tomorrow probably."

"Do," said Christine. She went into the drawing-room and sank into a chair. "Who ever heard of not saying good-by to one's fiancée?"

He saw that she was in her most teasing mood, and somehow this made him more serious.

"Perhaps," he said rather stiffly, "you think I carry out your instructions too exactly. Perhaps I show a more scrupulous devotion in public than you meant."

"Oh, no. It looked so well."

"It would not have looked so well for Linburne to take you home."

She clapped her hands. "Excellent," she said, "but you know it is not necessary to take that proprietary tone when we are alone."

"Even as a mere acquaintance I might offer you some advice," he said.

"I'm rather sleepy as it is," she returned, yawning slightly.

For the first time Riatt had a sense of crisis. He knew he must either save her, or leave her. He could not give her a little sage advice and abandon her. It would be like advising a starving man not to steal and going away with your pockets full. He could not say, "Have nothing to do with a selfish materialist like Linburne," when he knew better perhaps than any one how empty of any ideality or hope her relation to Hickson was bound to be. Yet on the other hand, he could not say, "Come to me, instead." He despised her method of life, distrusted her character, disliked her ideas, and was under no illusion as to her feeling for himself. If he had come to her without money she would have laughed in his face. What chance would either of them have under such circumstances? It was simple madness to consider it. And why was he considering it? Just because she looked lovely and wan, sunk in a deep chair in all her black and gold finery, just because her face had the lines of an Italian saint and her voice had strange and moving tones in it.

"Good-by," he said briefly.

She sprang up. "Good gracious," she said, "and are you going just like that? You know it is customary to extract a promise to write. At least to beg for a lock of the hair." (She drew out a golden lock, and let it crinkle back into place again.) "Or do you think you will remember me without it?"

"I'm not so sure I want to remember you."

"I hope you don't. It's the things you don't want to remember that you never can get out of your head."

"Good-by," he said again.

"Haven't you one nice thing to say to me before you go?"

"Not one."

"Wouldn't you at least admit that I had enlarged your point of view?"

"Aren't you going to shake hands with me?" he said.

She shook her head, and began to approach him. He felt afterward as if he had known exactly what she meant to do, and yet he seemed to

ALICE DUER MILLER

lack all power to prevent her—or perhaps it was will that was lacking. She came up to him, very deliberately put her arms about his neck, and, almost as tall as he, laid her head on his shoulder; and then murmured under his chin: "But you must never, never come back."

He stood like a rock under her caress; he did not make any answer; he did not attempt to undo the clasp of her arms. He was as impassive as a hunted animal who, in some terrible danger, pretends to be already dead.

It was a matter of only a few seconds. Then she dropped her arms, and he went away.

V

Running away is seldom a becoming gesture, yet it is one that should at least bring relief; but as Riatt went westward, he was conscious of no relief whatsoever. The day was bitter and gray, and, looking out of the window, he felt that he was about as flat and dreary as the country through which he was passing.

He sat a little while with the Lanes in their compartment.

"I suppose you'll be glad to get home and see George and Louise and the children," said Mrs. Lane, referring to some cousins of Riatt's about whom, it is to be feared, he had not thought for weeks.

Dorothy laughed. "What does he care for home-staying cousins when he is leaving a lovely creature languishing for him in New York?" she said.

"I doubt if Christine does much languishing," he returned, though the idea was not at all disagreeable to him.

"You two are the strangest lovers I ever knew," said Miss Lane.

Riatt wondered if that were an accurate description of them—lovers, though strange ones.

He left his old friends presently and went and sat in the observation-car. What, he wondered, had Christine meant by her last words, about never coming back? Never come back to annoy with his critical attitude? Never come back to watch her deterioration as Hickson's wife? Or never come back to disturb her peace of mind and heart by his mere presence? He debated all interpretations but the last pleased him most.

A bride and groom were in the car. The girl was not in the least like Christine. She was small and wore a pair of the most fantastic gray and black boots that Riatt had ever seen; but she was very blond and very much in love. Riatt hated both her and her husband. "People ought not to be allowed to show their feelings like that," he said to himself, as he kicked open the door leading to the back platform, with a violence that was utterly unnecessary.

Nor did things mend on his arrival at his home. His native town was naturally interested in his engagement; it showed this interest by keeping the idea continually before him. It assumed, of course, that he was going to bring his bride home. The rising architect of the community came to him with the assumption that he would wish to build her a more suitable house than that of his father, which, large and comfortable, had been constructed in the very worst taste of the early "eighties." No, Riatt found himself saying with determination, his father's house would be good enough for his wife. He thought the sentiment sounded rather well, as he pronounced it. But this did not solve his difficulties, for now it was but too evident that he must at least redecorate the old house; and he found himself, he never knew exactly how, actually in process of doing over a bedroom, bathroom and boudoir for Christine, just exactly as if he had expected her ever to lay eyes on them.

Mrs. Lane came to him with the suggestion that he would wish Christine to be one of the patronesses of the next winter's dances. The list was about to be printed. Max hesitated. "It would be a little premature to put her down as Mrs. Riatt, wouldn't it?" he objected. Mrs. Lane thought this was merely superstitious, and ordered the cards so printed without consulting him further.

Every one asked him what he heard from her, so that he actually stooped once or twice to invent sentences from imaginary letters of hers. He even went so far as to read the society columns of the New York newspapers, so that he might not be caught in any absurd error about her whereabouts. Such at least is the reason by which he explained his conduct to himself.

He was shocked to find that he was restless and dissatisfied. The only occupation that seemed to give any relief was gambling; or, as a mine-owning friend of his expressed it, in making "a less conservative and more remunerative investment of his capital." He spent hours every day hanging over the ticker in the office of Burney, Manders and Company—and this young and eager firm of brokers made more money in commissions during the first two weeks of his return than they had during the whole year that preceded it.

On the whole he lost, and Welsley, his mining friend, seeing this began to urge on him more and more the advisability of buying out the majority of stock in a certain Spanish-American gold mine. At first he always made the same answer: "You know as well as I do, Welsley, I would never put a penny into any property I had not inspected."

But gradually a desire to inspect it grew up in his mind. What would suit his plans better than a long trip, as soon as the breaking of his engagement was announced? A week at sea, two or three days on a river, and then sixty miles on mule-back over the mountains—there at least he would not be troubled by accounts of Christine's wedding, or assertions that she had looked brilliant at the opera.

He had been at home about two weeks, when her first letter came. So far the only scrap of her handwriting that he possessed was the formal release that she had given him the afternoon they became engaged, and which, for safe keeping doubtless, he always carried in his pocketbook, and which he sometimes found himself reading over—not as a proof that he could get out of his engagement, but rather in an attempt to verify the fact that he had ever got into it.

However unfamiliar with her writing, he had not the least doubt about the letter from the first instant that he saw it. No one else could use such absurd faint blue and white paper and such large square envelopes. As he took it up, he said to himself that it had never occurred to him that she would write, and yet he saw without any sense of inconsistency that he had looked for this letter in every mail. And yet, so perverse is the nature of mankind, that he opened it, not with pleasure, but with a sudden return of all his old terror of being trapped.

"Dear Max," it said. "I have been pretending so often to write to you for the benefit of my inquiring friends, that I think I may as well do it as a tribute to truth.

"How foolish that was—the night you went away! One gets carried away sometimes by the drama of a situation, without any relation to the facts, and the idea of parting forever from one's fiancé is rather dramatic, isn't it? I cried all night, and rather enjoyed it. Then in the morning when I woke up, everything seemed to have returned to the normal, and I could not understand what had made me so silly.

"Don't suppose that because you have gone, I am therefore freed from the disagreeable criticism of which you made such a speciality. Ned comes in almost every day to tell me that he does not approve of my conduct. I am not behaving, it appears, as an affianced bride should. Don't you like to think of Ned so loyally protecting your interests in your absence? His criticisms are, I suppose, based on the attentions of a nice little boy just out of college, who calls me 'Helen,' and writes sonnets to me which are to appear in the most literary of weeklies. Look out for them. They are good, and may raise your low estimate of my charms. The best one begins:

"When the blond wonder first on Paris dawned—

"Isn't that pretty?

ALICE DUER MILLER

"Write to me. At least send me a blank envelope that I may leave ostentatiously on my desk.

"Yours at the moment,
"CHRISTINE."

Riatt's first thought on laying down the letter was: "Hickson never in the world objected to any little poet just out of college, and she knows it very well. It's Linburne he is worried about—Linburne, whose name she does not even mention." And how absurd to attempt to make him believe she had cried all night. That was simply an untruth. Yet oddly enough, it came before his eyes in a more vivid picture than many a scene he had actually witnessed.

A few minutes later he went to the club and looked up the literary weekly of which she had spoken. There was no sonnet in it, but the issue of the next week contained it. Riatt read it with an emotion he could not mistake. It brought Christine like a visible presence before him. Also it made him angry, to have to see her like this, through another man's eyes. "Little whelp," he said, "to detail a woman's beauty in print like that! What does he know about it anyhow? I don't believe for one second she looked at him like that."

The sonnet ended:

She turned, a white embodiment of joy,
And looking on him, sealed the doom of Troy.

He was roused by a friendly shout in his ear. "Ho, ho, Max, reading poetry, are you? What love does for the worst of us!" It was Welsley, who snatched the paper out of his hand, running over the lines rapidly to himself: "Hem, hem, 'carnation, alabaster, gold and fire.' Some queen, that, eh? Have you had your dinner? Well, don't be cross. There's no reason why you shouldn't read verse if you like. And this young man is the latest thing. My wife says they are going to import him here to speak to the Greek Study Club."

"I shall be curious to hear him, if the Greek Club will ask me," said Max.

"Oh, you'll be in the East getting married," answered Welsley.

Strangely enough, it was with something like a pang that Max said to himself that he wouldn't be.

"Carnation, alabaster, gold and fire."

It was not a bad line, he thought.

After dinner, he felt a little more amiable, and so he sat down and wrote his first real letter to his fiancée.

"If we were really engaged, my dear Christine," he wrote, "you would have had a night letter long before this, asking you to explain to me just how it was that you did look on that amorous young poet. His verse is pretty enough, though I can't say I exactly enjoyed it. However, my native town thinks very highly of him, and intends to ask him to come and address one of our local organizations. If so, I shall have an opportunity of questioning him on the subject of the sources of his inspiration. 'Is Helen a real person?' I shall ask. 'Not so very,' I can imagine his replying. Ah, what would we both give to know?

"My friends here, stimulated by Dorothy Lane's ravishing description of you, have asked many times to see your picture. I am ashamed of my own carelessness in having gone away without obtaining one for exhibition purposes. Will you send me one at once? One not already in circulation among poets and painters. I will set it on my writing table, and allow my eyes to stray sentimentally toward it whenever I have people to dinner.

"By the way, the day I left New York I told a florist to send you flowers every day. We worked out quite an elaborate scheme for every day in the week. Did he ever do it?

"Yours, at least in the sight of this company,

MAX RIATT

In answer to this, he was surprised by a telegram:

"So sorry for absurd mistake. Entirely misunderstood source of the flowers. Enjoy them a great deal more now. Yes, they come regularly. A thousand thanks. Am sending photograph by mail."

Riatt did not need to ask himself from whom she had imagined they came. Not the poet, unless magazine rates were rising unduly. Nor Hickson, who failed a little in such attentions. No, it was Linburne—

and evidently Linburne's attentions were taken so much as a matter of course, that she had not even thanked him, nor had he noticed her omission.

He did not answer the telegram, nor did he acknowledge the photograph but, true to his word, he established it at once on his desk in a frame which he spent a long time in selecting. The picture represented Christine at her most queenly and unapproachable. She wore the black and gold dress, and the huge feather fan was folded across her bare arms. Every time he looked at it, he remembered how those same arms had been clasped round his own stiff and unbending neck. And sometimes he found the thought distracted his attention from important matters.

It was about the middle of February when he received one morning a letter from Nancy Almar. He knew *her* handwriting. She was always sending him little notes of one kind or another. This one was very brief.

"Clever mouse! So it knew a way to get out all the time!"

All day he speculated on the meaning of this strange message. Had Nancy discovered some proof of the nature of his engagement? Had Christine been moved by pity to tell Hickson the truth? On the whole he inclined to think that this was the explanation.

The next day he knew he had been mistaken. He had a letter from Laura Ussher—not the first in the series—urging him to come back at once.

"Max," she wrote, with a haste that made her almost indecipherable, "you must come. What are you dreaming of—to leave a proud, beautiful, impressionable creature like Christine the prey to so finished a villain as Linburne? You are not so ignorant of the ways of the world as not to know his intentions. Most people are saying you deserve everything that is happening to you. I try to explain, but I know you saw enough while you were here to be put upon your guard. Why don't you come? I must warn you that if you do not come at once you need not come at all."

Riatt had just come in; it was late in the afternoon. The letters were lying on his writing table; and as he finished this one, he raised his eyes and looked at Christine's picture.

He did not believe Laura's over-wrought picture. Christine was no fool, Linburne no villain. There was probably a little flirtation, and a good deal of gossip. But that would all be put a stop to by the announcement of Christine's engagement to Hickson. He did not even feel annoyed at his cousin's suggestion that he did not know his way about the world. He knew it rather better than she did, he fancied.

And having so disposed of his mail, he took up the evening paper which lay beneath it, and read the first headline:

Mrs. Lee Linburne to seek divorce: Wife of well-known multimillionaire now at Reno—

As he read this a blind rage swept over Riatt. He did not stop to inquire why if he were willing to give Christine up to Hickson he was infuriated at the idea of Linburne's marrying her; nor why, as he had allowed himself to be made use of, he was angry to find that he had been far more useful than he had supposed. He only knew that he was angry, and with an anger that demanded instant action.

He looked at his watch. He had time to catch a train to Chicago. He went upstairs and packed. He knew that what he was doing was foolish, that he would poignantly regret it, but he never wavered an instant in his intention.

He reached New York early in the afternoon. He had notified no one of his departure, and he did not announce his arrival. He went straight to the Fenimers' house—not indeed expecting to find Christine at home at that hour, but resolved to await her return.

The young man at the door, who had known Riatt before, appeared confused, but was decided.

Miss Fenimer, he insisted, was out.

Glancing past him Riatt saw a hat and stick on the hall table. He had no doubt as to their owner.

"I'll wait then," he said, coming in, and handing his own things to the footman, who seemed more embarrassed still.

Taking pity on him, Riatt said:

"You mean Miss Fenimer is at home, but has given orders that she won't see any one?"

Such, the man admitted, was the case.

"She'll see me," Riatt answered, "take my name up."

The footman, looking still more wretched, obeyed. Riatt heard him go into the little drawing-room overhead, and then there was a long pause. Once he thought he heard a voice raised in anger. As may be imagined his own anger was not appeased by this reception.

While he was waiting, the door of a room next the front-door opened and Mr. Fenimer came out. His astonishment at seeing Riatt was so great that with all his tact he could not repress an exclamation, which somehow did not express pleasure.

"You here, my dear Riatt!" he said, grasping him cordially by the hand. "Christine, I'm afraid—"

"I've sent up to see," said Max, curtly.

"Ah, well, my dear fellow," Mr. Fenimer went on easily, "come, you know, a man really can't go off in the casual way you did and expect to find everything just as he likes when he comes back. I have a word to say to you myself. Shall we walk as far as the corner together?"

To receive his dismissal from Mr. Fenimer was something that Riatt had never contemplated.

"I should prefer to wait until the footman comes down," he answered.

"No use, no use," said Mr. Fenimer, suddenly becoming jovial, "I happen to know that Christine is out. Come back a little later—"

"And whose hat is that, then?" asked Max.

It had been carelessly left on its crown and the initials "L.L." were plainly visible.

Mr. Fenimer could not on the instant think of an answer, and Riatt decided to go upstairs unannounced.

As he opened the drawing-room door he heard Christine's voice saying: "Thank you, I shall please myself, Lee, even without your kind permission."

The doors in the Fenimer house opened silently, so that though Christine, who was facing the door, saw him at once, Linburne, whose back was turned to it, was unaware of his presence, and answered:

"You ought to have more pride than to want to see a fellow who has made it so clear he doesn't care sixpence about seeing you."

Christine openly smiled at Max, as she answered: "Well, I do want to see him," and Linburne turning to see at what her smile was directed found himself face to face with Riatt.

Max made a gesture to the footman, and shut the door behind his hasty retreat, then he came slowly into the room.

"In one thing you are mistaken, Mr. Linburne," he said. "I do care whether or not I see Miss Fenimer."

Linburne was angry at Christine, not only for insisting on seeing Riatt, but for the lovely smile with which she had greeted him. He was glad of an outlet for his feelings.

He almost shrugged his shoulders. "An outsider can only judge by your conduct, Mr. Riatt," he answered. "And I may tell you that you have subjected Miss Fenimer to a good deal of disagreeable gossip by your apparently caring so little."

"And others by apparently caring so much," said Max.

Christine was the only one who recognized at once the fact that both men were angry; and she did not pour oil on the waters by laughing gaily. "You can't find any subject for argument there," she observed, "for you are both perfectly right. You have both made me the subject of gossip; but don't let it worry you, for my best friends have long ago accustomed me to that."

"I hope you won't think I'm asking too much, Mr. Riatt," said Linburne, with a politeness that only accentuated his irritation, "in suggesting that as your visit is, I believe, unexpected, and as mine is an appointment of some standing, that you will go away and let me finish my conversation with Miss Fenimer."

Max smiled. "Oddly enough," he said, "I was about to make the same request to you. But I suppose we must let Miss Fenimer settle the question."

Christine smiled like an angel. "Can't we have a nice time as we are?" she asked.

This frivolous reply was properly ignored by both men, and Riatt went on: "Don't you think you ought to consider the fact that Miss Fenimer and I are engaged?"

"Miss Fenimer assures me she does not intend to marry you."

"And may I ask if you consider that she does intend to marry you— that is if you should happen to become marriageable?"

"That is a question between her and me," returned Linburne.

Riatt laughed. "I see," he said. "The matrimonial plans of my future wife are no affair of mine?" And for an instant he felt his most proprietary rights were being invaded.

"Miss Fenimer is not your future wife."

"Well, Mr. Linburne, I hear you say so."

"You shall hear *her* say so," answered Linburne. "Christine," he added peremptorily, "tell Riatt what you have just been telling me."

There was a long painful silence. Both men stood looking intently at Christine, who sat with her head erect, staring ahead of her like a sphinx, but saying nothing. After a moment she glanced up at Max's face, as if she expected to find there an answer to her problem. She did not look at Linburne.

"Christine," said Max very gently, "what have you told Mr. Linburne?"

　　　　　　　　　ALICE DUER MILLER

"She has told me everything," answered Linburne impetuously, and then seeing by the glance that the two others exchanged that such was not the case, his temper got the best of him.

"Do you mean you've been lying to me?" he asked.

"Just what did you tell him, Christine?" said Riatt, finding it easier and easier to be calm and protecting as his adversary grew more violent.

Christine looked up at him with the innocence of a child. "I told him that we did not love each other, and that our engagement was really broken, but that no one was to know until March."

"Why did you tell him that?"

"It's the truth, Max—almost the truth."

"Almost the truth!" cried Linburne. "Do you want me to think you care something for this man after all?"

"In the simple section of the country from which I come," observed Riatt, "we often care a good deal for the people we marry."

Linburne turned on him. "Really, Mr. Riatt," he said, "you don't take an idea very quickly. You have just heard Miss Fenimer say that she did not love you and that she considered your engagement at an end."

"I heard her say she had told you that."

"You mean to imply that she said what was untrue?"

"I could answer your question better," said Riatt, "if I understood a little more clearly what your connection with this whole situation is."

"The connection of any old friend who does not care to see Miss Fenimer neglected and humiliated," answered Linburne, all the more hotly because he knew it was an awkward question.

Perhaps the young poet had not been so wrong in attaching the name of Helen to Miss Fenimer, for she sat now as calmly interested in the conflict developing before her, as Helen when she sat on the walls of Troy and designated the Greek heroes for the amusement of her newer friends.

"May I ask, Mr. Riatt, what rights in the matter you consider that you have?" Linburne pursued.

For Riatt, too, the question was an awkward one, but he had his answer ready. "The rights," he said, "of a man who certainly was once engaged to Miss Fenimer, and who came East ignorant that the engagement was already at an end."

Christine laughed. "Very neatly put," she said.

"Neatly put," exclaimed Linburne. "You talk as if we were playing a game."

"You have the reputation of playing all games well, my dear Lee," she returned. The obvious fact that she was enjoying the interview, made both men eager to end it—but, unfortunately, they wished to end it in diametrically opposite ways.

"Christine," said Linburne, "will you ask Mr. Riatt to be so kind as to let me have ten minutes alone with you?"

Riatt spoke to her also. "I will do exactly as you say," he said, "but you understand that if I go now, I shall not come back."

Christine smiled. "Is that a threat or a promise?" she asked, the sweetness of her smile almost taking away the sting of her words.

Seeing that she hesitated, Riatt went on: "Since I have come more than a thousand miles to see you, don't you think you might suggest to Mr. Linburne that he let me have my visit undisturbed?"

There was a long and rather terrible pause, terrible that is to the two men. Christine probably enjoyed every second of it. There was nothing in Linburne's experience of life to make him think that any woman whom he had honored with his preference was likely to prefer another man to himself. So the pause was terrible to him, not because he doubted what the climax would be, but because he felt his dignity insulted by even an appearance of hesitation. Max, on the other hand, was still a good deal in doubt as to her ultimate intentions.

It was to him, finally, that she spoke.

"Max," she said, "do you remember that while we were staying at the Usshers' we composed a certain document together?"

He nodded, and then as she did not continue, he opened his pocketbook and took out the release.

She made no motion to take it; on the contrary, she leaned back and crossed her hands in her lap.

"Yes," she said, "that's it. Well, you may stay, if you care to burn that scrap of paper."

It was now Max's turn to hesitate, for the decision of freedom or captivity was in his own hands; the crisis he had so recklessly rushed to meet was now upon him.

"What is in that paper?" asked Linburne, as one who has a right to question.

Christine was perfectly good-tempered as she answered: "Well, Lee, it still belongs to Mr. Riatt; but if he decides not to burn it, I promise to tell you all about it as we drink our tea."

"Do you promise me that, Christine?"

"Most solemnly, Lee." She looked up at Linburne, and before Max knew what he was doing he found he had dropped the paper into the fire.

Strangely enough, though the fire was hot, the paper did not catch at once, but curled and rocked an instant in the heat, before it disappeared in flame and smoke. Not until it was a black crisp did Christine turn to Linburne, and hold out her hand.

"Good-by, Lee," she said pleasantly. But he did not answer or take her hand. He left the room in silence.

When the door had shut behind him, Christine glanced at her remaining visitor. "And now," she said, "I suppose you are wishing you had not."

"What sort of a woman are you?" Riatt exclaimed. "Will you take any man that offers, me or Hickson, or Linburne or me again, just as luck will have it?"

"I take the best that offers, Max—and that's no lie."

The implied compliment did not soften Riatt. He went on: "If you and I are really to be married—"

"If, my dear Max! What could be more certain?"

"Since, then, we are to be married, you must tell me exactly what has taken place between you and Linburne."

"With pleasure. Won't you sit down?" She pointed to a chair near her own, but Riatt remained standing. "Shall we have tea first?"

"We'll have the story."

"Oh, it's not much of a story. Lee and I have known each other since we were children. I suppose I always had it in mind that I might marry him—"

"You loved him?"

"Certainly not. He always had too high an opinion of himself, and I used to enjoy taking it out of him—and making it up to him afterwards, too. I used to enjoy that as well. Sometimes, of course, he found the process too unbearable; and in one of his fits of anger at me, just after he left college, he went and blundered into this marriage with Pauline. She, you see, took him at his own valuation. His marriage seemed to put an end to everything between us—"

"You surprise me."

Christine laughed. "Ah, I was younger then."

"You kept on seeing him?"

"Naturally we met now and then. Sometimes he used to tell me how I was the only woman—"

"That is your idea of putting an end to everything?"

"Oh, if one took seriously all the men who say that—I did not think much about Lee's feelings for me, until my engagement was announced. Then it appeared that the notion of my marrying some one else was intolerable to him."

"A high order of affection," exclaimed Riatt. "He was content enough until there seemed some chance of your being happy."

"Perhaps he did not consider that life with you would promise absolute happiness, Max."

"I don't call that love. I call it jealousy."

At this Christine laughed outright. "And what emotion, may I ask, has just brought you here in such haste?"

The thrust went home. Riatt changed countenance.

"But I," he said, "never pretended to love you."

"Why then are you marrying me?"

"Heaven knows."

"I know, too," she answered, unperturbed by his rudeness, "and some day if you're good I'll tell you."

Her calm assumption that everything was well seemed to him unbearable. "I don't know that I feel very much inclined to chat," he said, turning toward the door. "I'll see you sometime tomorrow."

She said nothing to oppose him, and he left the room. Downstairs the same footman was waiting to let him out. To him, at least, Riatt seemed a triumphant lover, only as Linburne had long since heavily subsidized him, even his admiration was tinctured with regret.

As for Max, himself, he left the house even more restless and dissatisfied than he had entered it.

To be honest, he had, he knew, sometimes imagined a moment when he would take Christine in his arms and say: "Marry me anyhow." Such an action he knew would be reckless, but he had supposed it would be pleasant. But now there was nothing but bitterness and jealousy in his mood. What did he know or care for such people? he said to himself. What did he know of their standards and their histories? How much of Christine's story about Linburne was to be believed? What more natural than that they had always loved each other? Some one knew the truth—every one, very likely, except himself. But whom could he ask? He could have believed Nancy on one side as little as Laura on the other.

And as he thought this, he saw coming down the street, Hickson—a witness prejudiced, perhaps, but strictly honest.

For the first time in their short acquaintance, Hickson's face brightened at the sight of Riatt, and he called out with evident sincerity: "I am glad to see you."

"I came on rather unexpectedly."

"I'm glad you did. Quite right." Hickson stopped at this, and looked at his companion with such wistful uncertainty, that it seemed perfectly natural for Riatt, answering that look, to say:

"You may speak frankly to me, you know."

Ned took a long breath. "I believe that I may," he said. "I hope so, anyhow. I haven't had any one I could be frank with. Between ourselves, Fenimer is no good at all."

"What, my future father-in-law?"

"Is that what he is?" Hickson asked with, for him, unusual directness.

Riatt's affirmative was not very decided, and Ned went on:

"I can't even talk to Nancy about it. She's keen, but she does not understand Christine. She attributes the most shocking motives to her, and when I object, she says every one is like that, only I haven't sense enough to see it. Well, I never pretended to have as much sense as Nancy, but I see some things that she doesn't. I see, for instance, that there's something noble in Christine, in spite of—I beg your pardon for talking to you like this, but you must remember that I have known her a good deal longer than you have, and that in a different way perhaps I care for her almost as much as you do."

"I told you to speak frankly," answered Riatt. "What is it that Mrs. Almar says of Christine?"

At first Hickson refused to answer, but the suffering and anxiety he had been undergoing pushed him toward self-expression, and Riatt did not have to be very skilful to extract the whole story. Nancy had asserted that Christine had never intended for a minute to marry Riatt—that she had just used him to excite Linburne's jealousy to such a point that he would arrange matters so that he could marry her himself. For once Riatt found himself in accord with Nancy.

"Do more people than your sister think that?"

Hickson was not without his reserves. "Oh, I dare say, but I don't care about that sort of gossip. It's absurd to say she and Linburne are engaged. How can a girl be engaged to a married man?"

"We must move with the times, my dear Hickson," said Riatt bitterly.

"Linburne's no good," Ned went on, "not where women are concerned. He wouldn't treat her well if he did marry her. Why, Riatt," he added solemnly, "I'd far rather see her married to you than to him."

If Max felt disposed to smile at this innocent endorsement, he suppressed the inclination, and merely answered:

"You may have your wish."

"I hope so," said Ned. "But you mustn't go off to kingdom-come, and leave Linburne a clear field. He's a man who knows how to talk to women, and what with the infatuation she has always had for him—"

"You think she has always cared for him?" asked Max. He tried to smooth his tone down to one of calm interest, but it alarmed Hickson.

"I don't know," he returned hastily. "I used to think so, but I may be wrong. I thought the same thing about you at the Usshers'. She kept saying she wasn't a bit in love with you, but it seemed to me she was different with you from what she had ever been with any one else. I suppose I oughtn't to have said that either. Upon my word, Riatt, it is awfully good of you to let me talk like this! I can assure you it is a great relief to me."

His companion could hardly have echoed this sentiment. As he walked back alone to his hotel, he found that Hickson's words had put the last touches to his mental discomfort.

At first his own conduct had seemed inexplicable to him. Everything had been going well, he had been just about to be free from the whole entanglement, when an impulse of primitive jealousy and fierce masculine egotism had suddenly brought him to New York and bound him hand and foot. It had not been an agreeable prospect—to live among people whose standards he did not understand, with a woman whom he did not love. But, since his conversation with Hickson, his eyes were opened, and he saw the situation in far more tragic colors.

He *did* love her. He did not believe in her or trust her; he had no illusions as to her feeling for him, but his for her was clear—he loved her, loved her with that strange mingling of passion and hatred so often found and so rarely admitted.

He could imagine a man's learning, even under the most suspicious circumstances, to conquer jealousy of a woman who loved him. Or he could imagine having confidence in a woman who did not pretend love. But to be married to a woman whom you love, without a shred of belief either in her principles or her affection, seemed to Riatt about as terrible a prospect as could be offered to a human being.

There was just one chance for him—that Christine might be willing to release him. If she really loved Linburne, if there had been some sort of understanding between them in the past, if his coming had only precipitated a lovers' quarrel, then certainly Christine had too much intelligence to let such a chance slip through her fingers just on the eve of Linburne's divorce. Nor was she, he thought bitterly, too proud to stoop to ask a man to reconsider; nor did it seem likely, however deeply Linburne's vanity had been wounded, that he would refuse to listen.

With this in mind, as soon as he reached his hotel, he sat down and wrote her a letter:

My dear Christine:
"What was it, according to your idea, that happened this afternoon? I believed that for the first time I asked you to marry me, and that you, for the first time definitely accepted me. But as I think over your manner, I am led to think you supposed it was just a continuation of our old joke.

"Did you accept me, Christine? And if so, why? Why commit yourself to a marriage without affection, at the psychological moment when a man for whom you have always cared is about to be free?

"If you still need me in the game, I am ready enough to be of use, but I will not be bound to a relation unless you, too, consider it irrevocably binding.

Yours,
M.R.

He told the messenger to wait for an answer, but he thought that Christine would hardly be willing to commit herself on such short notice, or without an interview with Linburne.

But, within a surprisingly short interval, her letter was in his impatient hands.

Dear Max:
"I will not be so cruel as to leave you one moment longer in the false hope that your little break for freedom may be successful. Face the fact, bravely, my dear. I am going to marry you. We are both irrevocably bound—at least as

irrevocably as the marriage tie can bind nowadays. If this afternoon my manner seemed less portentous than you expected, that must have been because I have always counted on just this termination to our little adventure. You must do me the justice to confess that I have always told you so. As for Lee, in spite of Nancy (I suppose it was Nancy to whom you rushed for information from my very doorstep) I have never cared sixpence for him.

Yours till death us do part,
CHRISTINE

Max read the letter which was brought to him while he was at dinner. He put it into his pocket, finished an excellent salad, went to the theater, came back to the hotel and went to bed and to sleep rather congratulating himself on the fact that he had become callous to the whole situation, and that, so far as he was concerned, the crisis was past.

But of course it wasn't. With the rattle of the first milkcart, which in a modern city has taken the place of the half-awakened bird, he woke up, and if he had been in jail he could not have felt a more choking sense of imprisonment. There was no escape for him, no hope.

He got up and looked out at the city far below, all outlined like a great electric sign that said nothing. There must be some way of being free, besides jumping from the twelfth story window. He lit a cigarette, and stood thinking. Men disappeared every day; it could be done. What were the chances, he wondered, of being identified if he shipped as steward, or engineer for that matter, on a South American freighter?

It was full daylight before he found himself in possession of a possible scheme. He remembered the legend of a certain Saint, told him by his nurse in his early days. She had been beautiful, too beautiful for her religious ideals; the number of her suitors was distracting; so to one of them who had extravagantly admired her eyes she sent them on a salver.

Riatt did not intend sending Christine his worldly goods, but recognizing that they were the source of the whole trouble, he decided to get rid of the major part. The problem was simply to lose his money before the date set for the wedding. And that was not so difficult, after all. There were a number of people in the metropolis he thought who would give him every assistance.

The problem of getting it back again at some future time was more complicated, but even that he thought he could accomplish. He had made one fortune and he supposed he could some day make another.

The practical question was: What sum would make him impossible to Christine as a husband? Twenty thousand a year would be out of the question. But to be perfectly safe he decided to leave himself only fifteen thousand. He would begin operation as soon as the exchange opened in the morning. In the meantime what about that mine of Welsley's? There was an easy means of sinking almost any sum.

He took up the telephone and sent a telegram at once.

"Plans for my wedding prevent trip to mine. Have, however, decided after minute investigation here to invest $500,000 in it. Believe we shall make our fortunes."

He stood an instant with the instrument still in his hand. "Suppose the damned thing succeeds," he thought, "I shall be worse off than ever."

Then his faith returned to him. "Nothing of Welsley's ever did succeed," he thought; and with this conclusion he went back to bed and slept like a child.

VI

With his definite decision and unalterable plan of action, wonderful peace of mind had come to Riatt. He said to himself that he was now to have a few weeks—whatever time it should take him to lose his fortune decently—of being engaged to a woman whom, he now acknowledged, he passionately loved. He intended to make the best of it.

The next day as he walked up Fifth Avenue on his way to lunch with her, another inspiration came to him; it was not necessary to lose his money; spending it would be quite as effective. Acting on this idea, he went into a celebrated jeweler's shop, and with astonishing celerity chose, paid for and pocketed a string of brilliant pearls.

It was a present that might have made any man welcome—and Christine had never been accused of not being able to express herself when she wanted to—but Christine had already welcomed him for his changed demeanor; his brilliant smile and unruffled brow told her as soon as she saw him that he was a very different person from the tortured and irritable creature who had left her the preceding afternoon.

Never were two people more disposed to find each other and themselves agreeable, and Riatt was in process of clasping the pearls about Christine's neck (for she had had some unaccountable difficulty in doing it for herself) when the drawing-room door opened and Nancy Almar strolled in.

Her jaw did not actually drop at the scene that met her eyes, for that did not happen to be her method of expressing surprise, but her manner conveyed none the less an astonishment not very agreeable.

"Was I mistaken," she said, "in thinking I was to stop and take you to the Bentons'?"

"Quite right, my dear. Only Max's return has put everything else out of my head."

"What, you didn't ever expect him to come back?"

"You talk, Nancy, as if you had never heard that we were engaged."

"If you really are, Christine, why are the Linburnes being divorced?"

"Because they loathe each other, I imagine."

"What a changeable creature you are, Christine! It seems only the other day that you were crying your eyes out because Lee was engaged."

Without glancing at Max, Christine became aware that some of the gaiety had gone from his expression.

"Have you seen my pearls, dear?" she said.

It was a complete answer, so far as Nancy was concerned, for she was one of the women who can never harden herself to the sight of another woman's jewels.

"How beautiful, love," she answered. "If they were only a trifle larger they might be mistaken for your old imitation string." Then feeling that she could never better this, she took her departure.

"Oh, dear," sighed Christine, "do you think I shall ever get so superior that Nancy can't tease me when she says things like that?"

"Did you really cry, Christine?"

"The night you went away?"

"When you first heard of Linburne's engagement?"

She nodded at him, like a child who would like to lie its way out of a scrape.

"But then I often cry over trifles," she added.

"Like my going away?"

"Really, Max, you ought to be able to understand why I cried over Lee's engagement. It was Nancy who brought me the news, and she was so triumphant over it. She said every one would think he had been making a fool of me. You know she has the power of teasing me more than any one in the world—except, perhaps, you."

"I have a piece of news for you, Christine."

"Good or bad?"

"Indifferent, I think you would say. It's a scientific discovery."

"An invention, Max? Could I understand it?"

"I think you can if you make an effort."

"What is it?"

He put his arms suddenly about her. "I find I'm in love with you," he said, and added a moment later: "And just think that I've been engaged to you so long and that's the first time I've kissed you."

Christine with her head still buried on his shoulders murmured, "But it won't be the last."

Riatt's expression changed. "Not absolutely the last, perhaps," he answered with something that just wasn't a sigh.

She looked up at him. "That piece of indifferent news of yours—" she began.

"Didn't I describe it correctly?"

"It wasn't news to me."

"You mean you had already guessed that I loved you?"

"I've always known it."

"Always?"

"You can't think I would ever have let you go away at all, if I had not felt sure. And if you hadn't loved me, I couldn't have brought you back."

"I came back because—"

"Because the Linburnes were getting a divorce, and because Laura wrote you a letter. Do you fancy I had nothing to do with either of those events?"

And Riatt found himself answering almost in the word of Cyrano:

"Non, non, mon cher amour, je ne vous aimais pas."

The days that followed were the happiest that Riatt had ever known. Only those who have lived in a brief and agreeable present can understand the fullness of joy that he was able to extract from it. If he had been under sentence of death he could not have given less thought to the future. He gave himself up wholly to the two excitements of making love and losing money.

At first he prospered more at the former than the latter. For at first, for some time after he had acquired the stock of the mine, the reports from it grew more and more favorable and old friends came to him and begged him to allow them to take up a little of it. His curt refusal to all such propositions increased the impression that he knew he had a very good thing and meant to keep it all for himself.

But he did not have very long to wait for the turn of the tide. Within a few weeks he received a letter from Welsley, alarming only because its intention was so obviously to allay alarm. It appeared that a liberal revolution was threatened; the concession from the government then in power would not bear the scrutiny of an impartial witness such as our own State Department. If, in other words, the present government fell, the concession would fall, too.

"However," Welsley wrote cheerfully, "though the revolution has the support of the uneducated element of the population, which comprises most of the people, as they have neither arms, ammunition nor money, they can't do much, unless some fool in the north is induced to finance them. You could help us a lot by looking about and seeing if there is any danger of such a thing."

On receipt of this, Riatt instantly telegraphed to Welsley as follows:

"Count upon me. What is the name and address of the revolutionary agent here?"

The next day in a back bedroom of a down-town hotel, $10,000 changed hands between a slight, dark, very finished gentleman who spoke English with the slightest possible accent, and a tall, fine-looking young American whose name never appeared in the transaction. Within a month a shipment of arms had been smuggled into a certain South American country, with the result that the revolution was completely successful—as indeed it deserved to be. One of the first acts of the new government was to revoke the iniquitous concession of the San Pedro gold mine, made to "a group of greedy North American capitalists by the former corrupt and evil administration."

Riatt's bearing during this unhappy experience was universally praised. As he went in and out of his broker's office, not a trace of anxiety visible upon his countenance, men would nudge each other and whisper, "Did you ever see such nerve? He stands to lose a million."

The only moment of regret that he suffered was when one day, when things first began to look badly, he met Linburne and another man in Wall Street, and there was something subtly insulting and triumphant in the former's manner of condoling with him about the situation.

Rumors of it reached Christine. She liked the picture of Riatt's courage and calm, and hated the danger of his losing money.

"You're not risking too much, are you, Max?" she asked.

"Wouldn't you enjoy love in a cottage, Christine?" he answered.

She tried to make it clear to him how little such a prospect would tempt her, and gathered from the fact that he hardly listened to her reply that he felt confident there was no real danger.

With the success of the revolution, Riatt realized that his holiday was over, that he must tell Christine the truth and then retire to his old home and begin a new method of life on his decreased income.

It was now early April—a warm advanced spring—when he decided that the next day should see the end of his little drama. But, as we all know, it sometimes happens that those who set a mine are the most startled by the explosion; and Riatt, at an early breakfast (for he and Christine were going into the country for the day), with a mind occupied with the phrases in which he should bid her good-by and eyes lazily reading the newspaper, was suddenly startled beyond words by a short paragraph on the financial page. This stated in the baldest terms the failure of his brokers at home.

There was no country expedition for Riatt that day. He rushed downtown, leaving a short message for Christine, and by night he knew the worst, knew that the liabilities of the firm far exceeded any possible assets, knew positively that the comfortable sum he had intended to preserve for himself had been swept away, knew that he now really had to begin life over.

That night when he came back to his hotel, he understood for the first time that he had throughout been cherishing an unrecognized hope; that he had not been honest with himself, and that all the time beneath his great scheme had lain the belief that when the truth was known Christine would prefer him and his moderate income to Linburne and his wealth; that, in short, the great scheme had been all the time not a method of freeing himself, but a test of her affection.

Now any such possibility was over. Now he himself was facing the problem of mere existence—at least he would be as soon as he had collected his wits enough to face anything.

The next day, which was Sunday, he spent entirely with his lawyer. When he came back to his hotel, between the entrance and the elevator a figure rose in his path. It was Hickson.

"Riatt, I'm awfully sorry about this," he said.

"Thank you, Hickson. It's very decent of you to be," Max answered as cordially as he could, but he was tired and wanted to be let alone, and there was not as much real gratitude in his heart as there should have been. He did not ask Ned to sit down until he had explained with his accustomed simplicity that he had something of importance to say. Then Riatt let him lead the way to one of those remote and stuffy sitting-rooms in which all hotels abound. He saw at once that Hickson found it difficult to say what he had come to say, but Riatt was in no humor this time to help him out.

"I'm awfully sorry this has happened," Hickson went on, "not only on your account, but on Christine's. I mean that I did begin to hope that life with you meant peace and happiness for her—"

To cut him short, Riatt said quickly: "Now, of course, the marriage is out of the question."

Hickson's face brightened, as if the difficult words had been said for him. "You do feel that?" he said, nodding a little as if to encourage his friend.

Max did not answer at first in words; he laughed rather bitterly, and then after a pause he said, "Yes, Hickson, I do."

Ned was clearly relieved. "Of course," he said, "I did not know how that would be. But I own it did occur to me. The world is very censorious of poor Christine. Every one will say that she is the kind of woman who can't stick to a man in adversity. Yes, I assure you, Riatt, lots of these women who can't put down one of their motors without having nervous prostration will pillory Christine for breaking her engagement, unless—" he paused.

"I don't follow your idea, Ned."

Hickson sighed. "Why, as long as you recognize the impossibility of the marriage, couldn't you in some way make it appear that the breaking of the engagement came from you—as—if—"

"I see," said Riatt. There was a short silence, and then he asked in a tone that sounded perfectly calm to Hickson: "Is this a message from Christine?"

"Oh, no. Not a message from Christine, though she has been trying to communicate with you for two days. She can't see why you won't even answer her letters. I told her I would find you—"

"In fact, it *is* a message, or at least you are her messenger?"

"No, Riatt, at least not from her. I have a message for you, but not from her."

"From whom?"

"From Linburne. He has the greatest admiration for your power, abilities, in spite of any differences you may have had. He wants to offer you a position, only he felt awkward about doing it himself after what has taken place. He asked me to speak to you. It's a good salary, only it means going to Manchuria, no—"

"One moment," said Riatt. "These two messages, are they in any way connected?"

"I don't understand."

"Linburne's offer is not by any chance the reward for my giving Christine a suitable release?"

Hickson was really shocked. "How can you think such a thing, Riatt?"

"Where did you see Linburne?"

Hickson hesitated, but confessed after some protest that it had been at Christine's house.

"But you don't understand, you really don't," he said. "She has been distracted by your reverses, and not hearing from you she has turned to me, to Jack Ussher, to any one who could give her news and help you, as she imagined—"

"I understand quite enough," answered Riatt. "Thank Mr. Linburne for his kind offer and say I have other plans; and tell Christine she can have her absolution for nothing. I'll give her a letter that will put her right with every one." And walking to a desk:

"My dear Christine," he wrote. "As you are aware, I have lost everything I have in the world, and though I know that to a spirit like your own poverty could not alter love, I must own that I, more experienced in privation, find that the situation has had a somewhat chilling effect upon my emotions. In short, my dear, I cannot begin life over again hampered by a wife. Thanking you for the loyalty with which you have stood by me in this crisis, and wishing you every happiness in the future, believe me

Sincerely yours,
R.M. Riatt

He handed the note to Hickson. "I think that, taken externally, will effect a cure," he said. "Good night, Hickson. I'm dead tired, so you won't mind my going to bed. Oh, and I'm off tomorrow, so I shan't see you again. Good-by."

"Are you going home?" Hickson asked. But Max maintained a certain vagueness as to his plans, which Hickson, having accomplished his purpose, did not notice. He was very much pleased with the results of his diplomacy. No one could say a word against Christine now. It wasn't her fault if the engagement was broken. Riatt was a noble fellow—only, the noblest sometimes forgot these simple, practical details.

The next day Riatt paid his bill at the hotel and went away without leaving an address.

Few of us have driven past rows of suburban cottages, or through streets lined by city flats, without considering how easy it would be to sink one's identity and become part of a new unknown life. Riatt certainly had often thought of such a possibility and now he put his plans into operation. He took no great precautions against discovery, for he had no notion that any one would be particularly interested in knowing his whereabouts. But he allowed those at home to suppose he was working in New York, as he suggested to those in New York that he had very naturally gone home.

As a matter of fact, he had taken a position with a new company which was constructing aëroplanes for the market, into which in past times he had put a little money. He hired a small flat in Brooklyn, on the top floor, so that he had a glimpse of the harbor from his sitting-room windows. He spent the last of his ready money in buying out the dilapidated furniture of his predecessor; and then with the assistance of the janitor's wife, who gave him his breakfast and did what she called "redding up the place," he began to live on the slim salary that his new job gave him.

Every afternoon he would take the new machines out and fly at sunset over the sandy plains of Long Island, would dine cheaply at some neighboring restaurant, and would return to his flat about ten, go to bed early and be ready for work the next morning.

The only relaxation he allowed himself was the excitement of hating Christine, to which he now devoted a great deal of time and thought. It was the only thing that gave life any interest.

What was loss of money, after all, he said to himself, for an able-bodied man? He could bear that well enough, if his life had not been poisoned, if hope hadn't been taken from him. She had spoilt him for everything else. His success, if ever he should succeed, would not bring him what most men wanted of success—a companion and a home. He had nothing to work for, and yet nothing to do except work. It was all his own fault, he said; and blamed her all the more bitterly. He was glad, he thought, that he had made it impossible for her to have a final interview with him; and in his heart he could not forgive her for not having overcome the obstacles to a meeting which he had set up in the last frenzied days in New York.

"If I were of a revengeful disposition," he said to himself, "I should ask nothing better than that she should marry Linburne"; and he concluded that he was not revengeful because he found he did not want it. He made up his mind after the most prolonged consideration that a woman such as Christine exercised the maximum influence for evil; a thoroughly wicked woman could not help inspiring distrust, but a nature like hers had enough good to attach you and yet left you nothing to depend upon.

He read the papers, awaiting the announcement of her marriage, but found no mention of her name except once, toward the end of May, a short paragraph announcing that she had gone out of town for the season.

It was soon after he had read this that he came home earlier than usual and let himself into his little flat. The day had been successful, a new device in the engine was working well and the company had had a large order from abroad. And as usual, with the prospect of success had come to him a bitter sense of the emptiness of the future. He was thinking of Christine, and when he turned the switch of the electric light, there she was. She was sitting in a large shabby armchair, drawn close to the window, so that she could look out at the river. She had taken off her hat, and her hair shown particularly golden and her eyes looked brightly blue in the sudden glare of light.

"You're dreadfully late," she said, quite as if she had charge of his comings and goings. "I've been here hours and hours and hours."

Now that he actually saw her before him, it was neither love nor hate that he felt, but an undefinable and overmastering emotion that seemed to petrify him, so that he stood there quite silent with his hand on the switch.

"Well," she went on, "aren't you surprised to see me?"

He bent his head.

"Can you guess why I have come?"

He shook his head.

She looked a little distressed at this. "Then perhaps I've made a mistake in coming."

At this he spoke for the first time. "I should say that the chances were that you had," he said, and his tone was not agreeable.

The edge of his words seemed to give her back all her confidence. "Now, how strange that you should not know why I'm here! I've come, of course, to return your pearls." He saw now, between the laces of her summer dress that she was wearing them. "In common honesty I could hardly keep them." She put up her hands to the clasp, but it did not yield at once to her touch, and she looked up at him. "I think you'll have to undo it for me," she murmured, with bent head.

"I don't want them," he answered, with temper. "I never want to see them again."

"Nor me, either, perhaps?"

"Nor you either—perhaps."

She rose and approached him. "I'll keep them on one condition, Max—that you take permanent charge of both of us." Then seeing that she had produced no change in his expression, she came very close indeed. "There's no use in looking like a stone image, Max. It won't save you."

"Save me! And what is my danger?"

"I'm your danger, my dear."

"Not any longer, Christine."

"You mean you don't love me any more?"

"Not a bit."

At this she shifted her ground with admirable ease.

"In that case," she said cheerfully, "we can talk the whole subject over quite dispassionately."

"Quite, if there were anything to talk over."

"Only first," she said, "aren't you going to ask me to stay to dinner? It's very late, you know—"

"I don't dine here," he answered, "and I doubt if you would eat very much at the restaurant where I take my meals."

"Well, would you mind my going into the kitchen and making myself a cup of tea?"

He gave his consent, but evinced no intention of accompanying her. To see her like this, in his own home, where he had so often imagined her being and where she would never be again, was torture to him.

After an interval that seemed to him an eternity, she came back flushed and triumphant, carrying a tray on which were tea, toast and scrambled eggs.

"There," she said, "don't you think I've improved? Don't you think I'm rather a good housewife?"

The element of pathos in her self-satisfaction was too much for him. "I'm afraid I'm not in the mood either for comedy or for supper," he said.

Her face fell. "I thought you'd be so hungry," she observed gently. "But no matter. Sit down and we'll talk."

"I know of nothing to talk about," he returned, but he dropped reluctantly into a hard, stiff chair opposite her.

"I'll tell you what there is to talk about," said Christine. "Something that has never been mentioned in all the discussions that have been taking place. And that is my feelings."

"Your feelings," Riatt began, rather contemptuously, but she stopped him.

"No," she said, "you shan't say what you were going to. My feelings, my feelings for you. You've told me that you did *not* love me, that you despised me, that you *did* love me, but you've never asked how I felt to you."

"But you've made it so clear. You felt that, in default of anything else, I would do."

She leaned across the table and looked at him gravely. "Max," she said, "I love you."

He made no motion, not even one of contempt, and so she got up, and coming round the table, she knelt down beside him and put her arms tightly about him. Still he did not move, except that his hands, which had been hanging at his sides, now gripped the edges of the chair with the rigidity of iron, and he said in a voice which sounded even in his own ears like that of a total stranger:

"What folly this is, Christine!"

"Why is it folly?"

"If you had said this six weeks ago, while I still had enough money to—"

"If I had said it then you wouldn't have believed me." He looked at her; it was true.

"But now," she went on rapidly, "you must believe me. If I come now to live with you and work for you, no one can accuse me of mercenary motives—not even you, Max. I shan't get anything from the bargain but you, and that is all I want."

"This is madness," said Riatt, trying not very sincerely to free himself.

"Yes, of course it's mad, like all really logical things," she answered. "But that's the way it's going to be. I love you, and I am going to stay with you."

"I couldn't let you," he said. "I couldn't accept such a sacrifice."

"A sacrifice, Max. That's the first really stupid thing I ever heard you say. It isn't a sacrifice; it's a result, a consequence of the fact that I love you. It isn't a question of my doing it, or your letting me. It simply can't be otherwise. The other things I used to value—parties and pretty clothes and luxuries—they were a sort of game I played because I did not know any other. But only part of me was alive then. I was like a blind person; and they were my stick; but now that I can see, the stick is just in my way. It isn't silly and romantic to believe in love, Max. The hardest-headed, most practical people believe in it—every one who has any sense really believes in it, when they find it. To be poor, to be uncomfortable—it's a price, but a small one to pay for love. Isn't that true—true, at least, as far as you're concerned?"

"Oh, yes, as far as I'm concerned—"

"Then what right have you to think it's not true to me? Don't be such a moral snob, Max. If love's the best thing in the world for you, it's ever so much more so for me—I need it more."

"Nobody could need it more than I do," he answered, suddenly clasping her to him.

"It's the way it's going to be, anyhow," she murmured.

"I can't let you go," he said, as if arguing with an unseen auditor.

She nodded in a somewhat contracted space. "That's it," she announced. "It has to be."

It was only a few days later that Nancy Almar, driving past a well-known house-furnishing shop on her way home to tea, was surprised to observe her brother standing, with a salesman at his elbow, in trancelike contemplation of a small white enameled ice-box. With her customary decision, Nancy ordered her chauffeur to stop, and entering the shop by another door she stood close beside Hickson during his purchase of the following articles: the ice-box, an improved coffee percolator and a complete set of kitchen china of an extremely decorative pattern.

"Bless me, Ned," she said suddenly in his ear, "might one ask when you are going to housekeeping, and with whom?"

There was no denying that Ned's start was guilty, and his manner confused as he answered, "Oh, they're not for me—"

The salesman who, perhaps, lacked tact, or possibly only wanted to get away to wait on another customer, said at this point:

"And the address, sir? I have the name—Mrs. Max Riatt."

"Riatt married!" cried Nancy. "But to whom? I thought he had nothing left in the world."

"He hasn't," answered Ned, hastily scribbling the address on a card and handing it to the man.

"Oh, then he's married some one who loves him for himself alone, I know. That faithful sleek-headed girl from his home town. Won't Christine be angry when she hears it! She always likes her old loves to pine a long time before they console themselves. Let us go and tell her. Or is she away still?"

A rather sad smile lit up Hickson's countenance as he followed his sister to her motor. "I think she knows it," he said.

Nancy put her hand on his arm. "Oh, dear, darling Ned," she said. "Get in and drive home with me and tell me all about it. I knew he really never cared for Christine. She dazzled and distressed him in about equal proportions. And yet I doubt if Miss—Whatever-Her-Name-Was—will be very exciting—"

"It is not Miss Lane, who, by the way, I like and admire very much," said Ned, firmly.

"Who is it? Some one I know?"

"Yes, you know her."

Something in his extreme solemnity transferred the idea to her.

"You don't mean that Christine—"

He nodded. "I was at their wedding yesterday."

"And where are they?"

"That's it, Nancy. They're living in a flat and they have no servant—"

His sister leaned back and laughed heartily, and then composing her countenance with an effort, she said: "My poor dear! But it's really all for the best. She won't stay with him six months."

"Nancy! She'll stay with him forever."

"Where is this flat?"

"I've promised not to tell. They don't want to be bothered by all of us."

"They want to conceal their deplorable situation, of course. Well, my dear, I can wait. Six months from now I'll ask them to dine to meet Linburne. Christine's dresses will be a little out of fashion, and they'll come in a trolley car, and she'll have a veil over her head—"

"Six months from now Riatt may be on the way to making a nice little sum. He has a very good thing, he thinks."

"He'd better be quick about it. A flat in summer! Oh, the cinders on the window-sill, and the sun on the roof, and the knowledge that all of us are going out of town to lawns and lakes—He'd better be quick, Ned."

The motor had stopped before the door of Nancy's little house which was arrayed in its summer dress of red and white awnings, and red and white window boxes. The footman had rung the bell, and was waiting with his eye on the front door, so as to catch the right second for opening the door of the motor.

"Nancy," said her brother, with real horror in his tone, "you talk as if you wanted her to fail."

"I do. I do, of course."

"Why? Do you hate her?"

Nancy nodded. "Yes, I hate her now. I didn't used to."

"It seems to me this is just the moment to admire her. It may be foolish, but surely what she has done is noble, Nancy."

The hall door opened and simultaneously the door of the motor, and Nancy, putting out one foot, said over her shoulder:

"Oh, Ned, what a goose you are! Don't you know any woman would have done what she's done, if she had the chance—the real chance?"

She ran up the steps and into her house, leaving her brother staring after her in amazement.

A Note About the Author

Alice Duer Miller (1874–1942) was an American novelist, poet, screenwriter, and women's rights activist. Born into wealth in New York City, she was raised in a family of politicians, businessmen, and academics. At Barnard College, she studied Astronomy and Mathematics while writing novels, essays, and poems. She married Henry Wise Miller in 1899, moving with him in their young son to Costa Rica where they struggled and failed to open a rubber plantation. Back in New York, Miller earned a reputation as a gifted poet whose satirical poems advocating for women's suffrage were collected in *Are Women People?* (1915). Over the next two decades, Miller published several collections of stories and poems, some of which would serve as source material for motion picture adaptations. *The White Cliffs* (1940), her final published work, is a verse novel that uses the story of a young women widowed during the Great War to pose important questions about the morality of conflict and patriotism in the leadup to the United States' entrance into World War II.

A Note from the Publisher